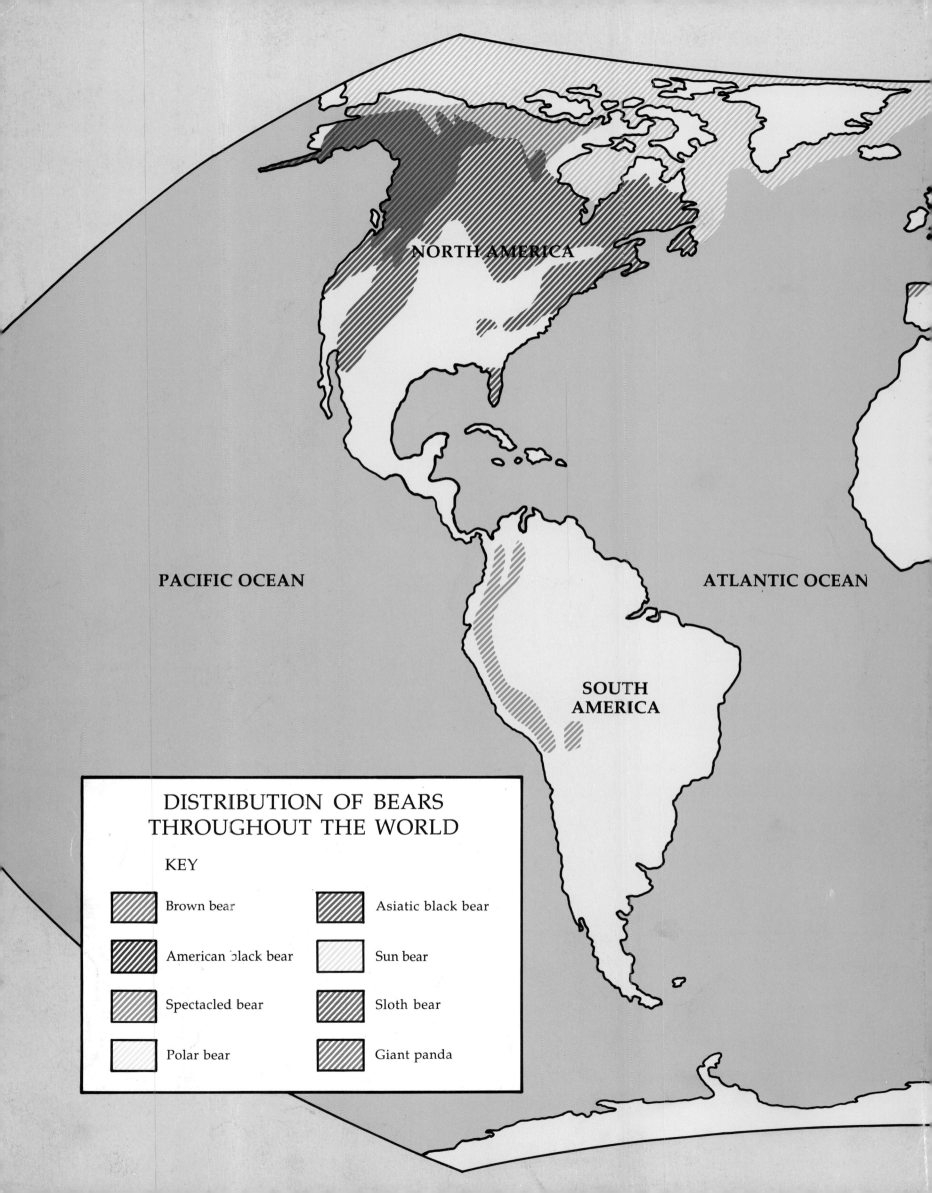

PACIFIC OCEAN

ATLANTIC OCEAN

NORTH AMERICA

SOUTH
AMERICA

DISTRIBUTION OF BEARS
THROUGHOUT THE WORLD

KEY

Brown bear

Asiatic black bear

American black bear

Sun bear

Spectacled bear

Sloth bear

Polar bear

Giant panda

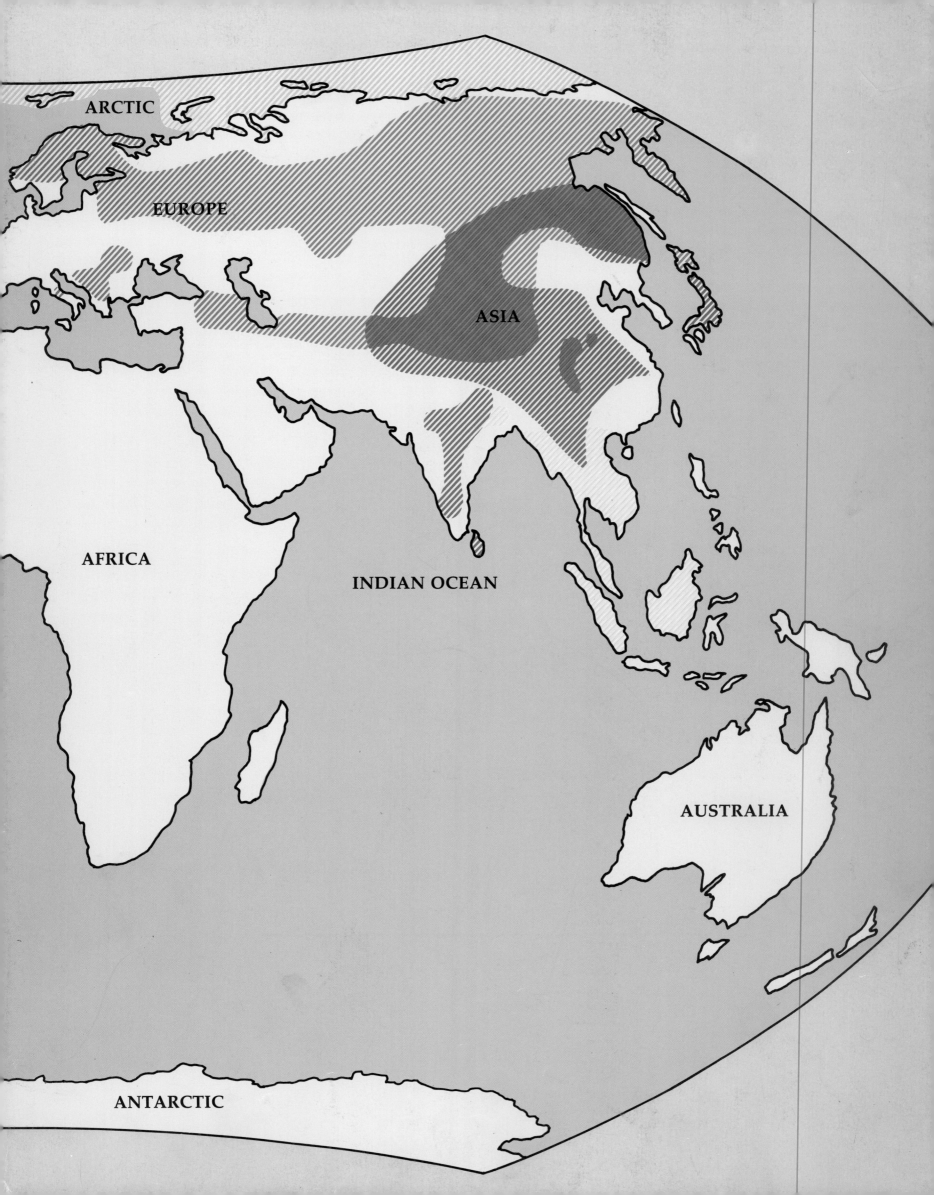

For Thomas
H. G.

For Chris
A. B.

Text copyright © 1993 by Helen Gilks
Illustrations copyright © 1993 by Andrew Bale
First American edition 1993 published by Ticknor & Fields.
A Houghton Mifflin company, 215 Park Avenue South, New York, New York 10003.
First published in Great Britain by David Bennett Books Ltd

Manufactured in Singapore

Book design by Andrew Bale and Roger Hands
Text of this book is set in Palatino
The illustrations are colored pencil
Consultant: Dr Jeff Carr, Huddersfield New College

10 9 8 7 6 5 4 3 2 1

Helen Gilks would like to thank Jeff Carr, who has worked
with bears in Alaska, Finland, Romania, and Italy, for his
considerable help and guidance with this book,
and Chris Servheen, Grizzly Bear Recovery Co-ordinator
with the US Fish and Wildlife Service, for kindly
reading the text.

Library of Congress Cataloging-in-Publication Data

Gilks, Helen.
  Bears / written by Helen Gilks ; illustrated by Andrew Bale. —
1st American ed.
     p.   cm.
  Summary: Describes the physical characteristics, habits, and
behavior of different kinds of bears, including the polar bear,
American black bear, sloth bear, and giant panda.
  ISBN 0-395-66899-9
  1. Bears—Juvenile literature. [1. Bears.] I. Bale, Andrew,
ill. II. Title.
QL737.C27G49   1993
599.74'446—dc20   92-37693
                                                   CIP
                                                   AC

BEARS

Written by
HELEN GILKS

Illustrated by
ANDREW BALE

TICKNOR & FIELDS

NEW YORK

1993

CONTENTS

Polar bear
(Ursus maritimus)
Head and body: 6.5-8.5 feet
Shoulder height: 4.5-5.5 feet

American black bear
(Ursus americanus)
Head and body: 4.5-6 feet
Shoulder height: 2-3 feet

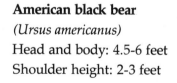

Brown bear
(Ursus arctos)
Head and body: 5.5-9.5 feet
Shoulder height: 3-5 feet

Every animal and plant has a scientific name which is the same all over the world. Whatever language scientists speak, they use the scientific name so they can be sure they are speaking about the same animal or plant, and can compare their discoveries about it. Scientific names are made up of two words. The first is the group to which the animal belongs. You can see that many of the bears are *Ursus*, which means "bear" in Latin. The second word identifies the particular type, or species, of bear.

Giant panda
(Ailuropoda melanoleuca)
Head and body: 4-5 feet
Shoulder height: 2.5-3 feet

Asiatic black bear
(Ursus thibetanus)
Head and body: 4-6 feet
Shoulder height: 2-3 feet

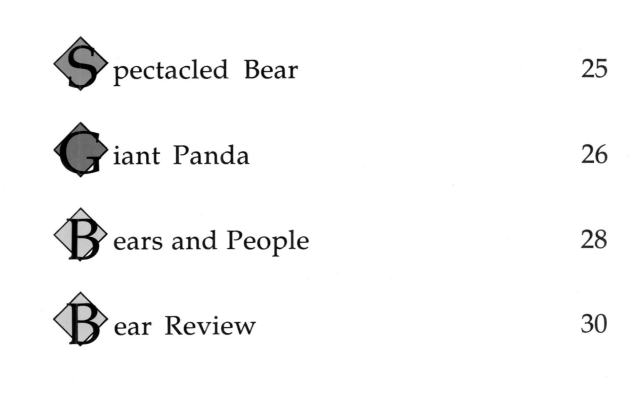

Sloth bear
(Melursus ursinus)
Head and body: 4.5-6 feet
Shoulder height: 2-3 feet.

Spectacled bear
(Tremarctos ornatus)
Head and body: 4.5-6 feet
Shoulder height: 2-3 feet

Sun bear
(Helarctos malayanus)
Head and body: 3.5-4.5 feet
Shoulder height: 2-2.5 feet

Bear Facts

Bears live in a variety of habitats, from the rainforests of Asia to the ice floes of the Arctic. There are eight different kinds of bears in the world, and, even though their habitats are very different, they have many things in common. Bears have few enemies apart from human beings, and can live as long as thirty years in the wild.

American black bear

Bears belong to a group of animals called carnivores (meat-eaters). In fact, they eat many different kinds of food, depending on what is available, and usually only a small part of what they eat is meat. Their teeth suit their varied diet. Bears use their sharp, pointed front teeth for biting and their flatter back teeth for crushing and grinding plants.

European brown bear

Bears are good climbers and the smaller species spend much of their time in trees. Large bears, such as grizzlies, climb less often.

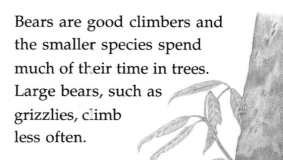

sun bear

Bears that live where food is difficult to find in winter sleep through the cold months in dens. Pregnant females give birth during this time. Bears live alone, except for females raising cubs. Male bears, which are called boars, have nothing to do with the cubs, or with other adult bears, except during mating season.

*wet nose to increase
sensitivity to smells*

*eyes and ears quite small
compared with size of body*

*use smell more than sight
when searching for food*

European brown bear

Bears are mammals. Like human beings, they give birth to young which feed on milk for the first few months of their lives. A female bear, or sow, has four nipples for cubs to drink from.

*thick furry coat
for warmth*

Bears can stand on their back legs. This gives them a better view of their surroundings and helps them pick up scents more easily.

*very large,
flat paws*

*five long claws
on front paws, used
for digging, climbing
or catching prey*

9

Polar Bear

Polar bears live in one of the coldest places on Earth—
the ice floes of the Arctic Ocean. They are the largest
carnivores that live on land and can be very dangerous.

*Under the polar bear's skin
are several inches of a fat,
which is called blubber. Blubber
helps keep the bear warm.*

*The polar bear's fur coat blends perfectly
with its snowy surroundings. Although
the coat looks white, each hair is
actually transparent and hollow.
The sun's light, reflecting off
the fur, makes it appear
white. Underneath the
coat, the polar bear's skin
is black, to absorb as
much heat as possible.
A polar bear's fur is
extremely warm and
Inuit people use it
to make boots,
mittens, and
sleeping mats.*

10

A polar bear is an excellent swimmer and can easily swim 50 miles without a rest. Its huge front paws are slightly webbed. Bears use their front paws like oars to push themselves through the water. They use their smaller back paws for steering.

A polar bear has very small ears for its size. Larger ears would stick out and freeze more easily.

The polar bear's sense of smell is very keen. A bear can pick up the scent of a seal several miles away, and it can sniff out seal pups that are in dens deep under the ice.

The polar bear's main food is seals. The bears often catch them at breathing holes the seals have made in the ice. As the seal comes up to breathe, the polar bear attacks.

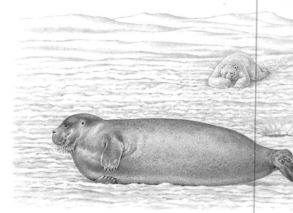

To catch a seal on the ice, a polar bear gradually creeps toward it. The bear keeps its body close to the ground, stopping if the seal opens its eyes, until the bear is near enough to charge. Some Inuit people say they have seen a polar bear cover the black tip of its nose with a paw to avoid being seen.

The huge paws are often 12 inches wide and 18 inches long. Furry pads on the soles of their feet help polar bears grip the ice, and their sharp claws help them catch slippery seals.

11

Polar bears travel hundreds of miles each year. Male bears travel all year, but pregnant females go into dens during the winter to give birth to their cubs, which are usually twins. Polar bears are very protective mothers and look after their cubs for almost three years.

In late autumn, a pregnant polar bear digs a den in a bank of snow. A long tunnel leads up to the den so the warmer air in the den does not escape. Snow is a good insulator and the air in the den stays warmer than the air outside.

The cubs are about the size of guinea pigs when born, and could not possibly survive outside. They keep warm with their mother in the den, drinking her milk and growing fast. In two months, the cubs are twenty times their birth weight and better able to survive the cold outside the den.

In April, the female emerges cautiously from the den. Once she has made sure that there is no danger, she encourages her cubs to come out. The mother bear is careful to keep away from other polar bears, which might attack her cubs if given the chance.

The female bear does not eat while she is in the den. She loses a great deal of weight during this time and, when she emerges in the spring, she is thin and hungry.

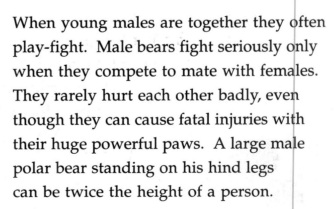

Although some bears live all year round on the ice, others spend the summer on land, eating plants, seaweed, and whatever else they can find. In the autumn, they wander back toward the sea. When it freezes over they can cross onto it to hunt seals. At this time of year, large numbers of bears pass a town called Churchill, in Canada, on their way back to the sea. Many tourists watch the bears from tundra buggies.

When young males are together they often play-fight. Male bears fight seriously only when they compete to mate with females. They rarely hurt each other badly, even though they can cause fatal injuries with their huge powerful paws. A large male polar bear standing on his hind legs can be twice the height of a person.

13

Brown Bear

Brown bears live in more parts of the world than any other kind of bear. They live in North America, Europe, and Asia. In some areas, brown bears grow as large as polar bears; in other places, they are less than half that size. The color of their coats also varies greatly, ranging from light brown to almost black. Because of these differences in size and color, people used to think there were many different species, not just one.

The biggest brown bears live in the forests of British Columbia and Alaska, and in the Kamchatka peninsula of Siberia. These bears are very large, probably because they eat a lot of fish, which is rich in protein, and weigh between 400 and 1,215 pounds. In summer, the bears gather along rivers and lakes to catch salmon which are swimming upriver to lay their eggs.

All brown bears have a muscly hump on their backs. The grizzly's is the biggest one.

grizzly bear

In the Arctic, the Rockies, and the Pacific coastal mountain ranges of North America live smaller brown bears, known as "grizzlies." People first called them grizzlies because the tips of their brown hairs are gray or grizzled.

14

Grizzlies inhabit open countryside, along the edges of forests or in the tundra. They weigh between 200 and 900 pounds. The grizzly's diet consists mainly of plant food—grass, leaves, roots, berries, and seeds—but it also eats carrion (dead animals), insects, and small mammals such as ground squirrels. Like all brown bears, it rarely attacks large animals, except when it finds one that is old, sick, or wounded; however, because grizzlies will sometimes attack domestic cattle and sheep, most farmers do not want bears living close to their animals. Grizzlies were once widespread across the prairies of North America but, as farmers moved in with livestock, the bears were driven out.

grizzly bear

long front claws for digging

There were once many brown bears living in Europe, but now they are numerous only in the forests of Scandinavia, Russia, and parts of eastern Europe. A few still live in Spain, the Pyrenees, and the Abruzzi mountains of Italy.

European brown bears are small, weighing 100 to 255 pounds, and eat many kinds of plants and small animals. In Europe, brown bears seldom attack people. They seem to have learned to keep away from human beings.

Like other brown bears, a European brown bear molts, or loses its old coat, in early summer. Underneath the old hair is a new coat of short, glossy fur.

Each brown bear lives within an area of land called a home range, which may overlap the ranges of other bears. Bears sometimes mark their ranges by scratching on trees and urinating. Most of the time, bears avoid contact with each other, but when a female is ready to mate she gives off special scents which attract males. Several males may compete to mate with one female. Usually the largest and strongest succeeds.

The boar is usually larger than the sow.

Before mating, a pair will play together and the female may rebuff the male several times. A male and female do not form a permanent pair and each one may mate with several others. Even though a female's eggs have been fertilized, they do not start to grow right away.

In autumn, bears gorge themselves on berries, putting on as much as 3.3 pounds of fat a day. When the weather turns colder, the bears dig a den or find a hollow cave or hole in a tree. There, they sleep through the winter months, living off their own fat. During this time, which may be as long as five months, they do not eat, drink, or pass any waste. Their body temperature drops and their heartbeat slows down. When a pregnant female goes into her den, the fertilized eggs inside her start to grow. If she has not built up enough fat reserves, the eggs do not develop.

16

Occasionally, people are attacked by bears. In North America, many people go camping or hiking in areas where there are brown bears. Although bears will usually disappear as soon as they hear or smell a human, they can be dangerous if they are surprised. Hikers should attach small bells to their backpacks to warn bears of their approach, and should never try to touch or feed a bear.

Bears have a keen sense of smell and like different kinds of food, so they will sometimes explore garbage dumps and raid camps and cabins. Campers in bear country should not cook near the tent where they sleep, and should keep their food in special barrels or hung high in the trees, out of the reach of bears. If people are careful, dangerous incidents with bears can be avoided.

Bears usually live alone, so they do not need to communicate as much as animals, such as wolves and lions, that live in packs. It can be difficult for a person to know what a bear is going to do. A bear standing on its back legs moving its head from side to side may seem threatening, but it is often only trying to get a better view or scent of something. An aggressive bear will often put its head down and its ears back just before an attack. People should always avoid looking a bear in the face at close quarters and should never run away if one threatens to charge. Instead, a person should avoid eye contact, then roll up into a ball and lie still.

The baby brown bears are born in the den. There may be one or two, or as many as four cubs, each one tiny and helpless. Bear milk is many times richer in fat than human milk and the cubs grow very fast. When they are about two months old they are ready to leave the den with their mother. She rears the cubs on her own. The father has nothing to do with them.

A female bear will fiercely defend her cubs from enemies. For the first few months after they leave the den, the cubs' lives are in danger. They can be killed easily by other bears, mainly males who want to mate with the mother, and also by predators such as wolves.

Bear cubs learn survival skills from their mothers. They learn what kinds of food to eat, where and how to make their dens, and how to behave with other bears. Cubs raised in captivity can never survive in the wild because they have not learned these necessary skills.

Bear cubs are very playful and their mother is tolerant. She calls to them with grunting sounds. When she wants to stop them doing something she may swipe at them with her huge paws.

If they survive, the cubs will spend the next winter in their mother's den. The following summer, the mother bear usually chases her cubs away, forcing them to live on their own. Soon she will mate again and have new cubs.

Cubs in the same litter can be different colors.

American Black Bears

American black bears are the most common
bears in North America. They live in forests
over much of the continent and are good
climbers. Black bears are not always black;
some are brown or even cream-colored.

There are black bears with very
pale fur on the west coast of British
Columbia, in Canada. They are
known as Kermodes bears, after the
scientist who first described them.

In the heat of the summer,
bears may cool off by lying
in water. Black bears are
excellent swimmers.

In May and June, when the hungry bears emerge from
their dens, food is often scarce. Black bears will strip
bark from trees such as the Douglas fir to get at the soft
sapwood. Forestry companies in America sometimes
pay hunters to shoot the bears, because of the millions
of dollars of damage caused to their trees. One bear
can peel up to fifty trees in a night. Recently, some
foresters have tried to limit the damage by putting out
food for the bears, rather than shooting them.
So far these experiments have proved successful.

The black bear has short, curved claws, which help it climb trees.

Bear cubs enjoy playing, resting, and sunbathing in trees.

All bears like honey. A bear can rip a nest apart, ignoring the angry bees. In areas where bears live, beekeepers often place their hives high up on poles where bears cannot reach them, or surround them with an electric fence.

If alarmed, black bears climb trees. A mother sends her cubs up the tree and then follows them or stays on the ground to face the danger.

Bears scratch themselves against trees. Sometimes they do this to leave scent marks to warn other bears, but sometimes just to relieve an itch from parasites such as ticks, fleas, or lice.

21

Sun Bear

The sun bear is the smallest of all bears. It lives in the jungles of Malaya, Indonesia, Burma, Thailand, and India. It is active mainly at night and rests during the day on a platform of branches, which it makes high in the trees. The sun bear does not need to go into a den over winter because its forest home is warm all year round, and food is seldom scarce. Local people sometimes keep sun bears as pets, but very little is known about their life in the wild. The sun bear takes its name from the yellowish crescent on its breast.

The sun bear is a skillful climber. The soles of its paws are bare, which helps it grip trees.

This sun bear is licking honey from its paw with its long tongue.

short fur coat

The sun bear uses its claws to tear open wood to find insect nests, and licks up the insects with its long tongue. Its favorite food is honey, and it also eats fruit, eggs, and small creatures such as lizards, snails, and rodents.

Sun bears can do a large amount of damage in coconut plantations. They often climb to the top of a coconut palm and eat the heart, or bud, which kills the tree.

Sloth Bear

The first Europeans to see this bear believed it was
a type of sloth because of its ability to hang upside-
down from branches. Even though it was
soon identified as a bear, the name "sloth"
stuck. It lives in the forests of India,
Sri Lanka, and Nepal and has a pale
Y-shaped marking on its chest.

*long, shaggy hair,
especially over
its shoulders*

A mother sloth bear sometimes
carries her cubs on her back.
They cling to her shaggy hair
and, if frightened, they bury
their faces in her fur.

*very long claws
for digging*

The sloth bear eats mostly termites, using its long claws
to break through the walls of their nests. It forms its long tongue and lips
into a tube, blows away the dust, and sucks up the insects. This is a very noisy
process and can be heard more than 325 feet away. The bear has a gap between
its front teeth which allows it to suck in the termites, and the roof of its mouth
is hollowed and tubelike.

Asiatic Black Bear

The Asiatic black bear lives in the forests of many countries throughout Asia. It has several different names, including Himalayan black bear and moon bear, because of the white marking on its chest. Its scientific name, *Ursus thibetanus*, means "bear of Tibet." The black bears that live in cold regions go into dens during the winter. The others stay active all year round.

The black bear can stand and walk on its hind legs. Some people believe that this explains the origin of the stories about the abominable snowman.

mane of long hair over shoulders and neck

Asiatic black bears climb trees to eat the fruit, and also strip bark from them to get at the sapwood below. This damages the trees, and, in Japan, foresters often shoot the bears.

short, strong claws

Many black bears are killed each year because their gall bladders, paws, hides, and meat can be sold for a large amount of money. The gall bladder is used as medicine in some Asian countries.

24

Spectacled Bear

The spectacled bear, which lives in the foothills of the Andes mountains, is the only bear found in South America. It has a very shaggy, dark coat, and light markings around its eyes, which look like glasses and give it its name.

Each bear has different markings around its eyes.

Not much is known about the bear's behavior in the wild— one scientist spent seven years trying to study them and saw bears only eight times! No one knows how many spectacled bears survive.

The spectacled bear is a superb climber. Its favorite food is fruit, and it may spend several days feeding in the same tree. It also eats plants called bromeliads, stripping off the tough outer leaves to get at the soft base and heart.

Because the bears sometimes raid crops and attack livestock, local people often shoot them on sight.

25

Giant Panda

The giant panda lives only in the bamboo forests on the mountains of central China. It is one of the rarest animals in the world—fewer than 1,100 survive. Although the giant panda looks like a bear, scientists used to think it was more closely related to the raccoon. Biological tests carried out a few years ago showed that it is a member of the bear family.

The giant panda has a large head because of the huge muscles needed to chew so much bamboo.

In the wild, a giant panda feeds almost entirely on bamboo. As it eats, the bear usually sits on its haunches holding the bamboo with its paws. An extra digit on its front paws works like a thumb and helps it to grip the stems. The giant panda peels off the bamboo's tough outer skin to get at the juicy center.

Bamboo is not very nutritious, so a giant panda spends up to fourteen hours a day eating huge quantities of it—up to 85 pounds a day. Most of the bamboo passes, only partly digested, straight through the bear into its droppings.

About once every forty years, bamboo plants flower and form seeds. When this happens, all the plants over a large area die and it is several years before new ones grow. In the mid 1970s and again in 1983, two kinds of bamboo flowered, and many giant pandas could not find enough to eat, so died of starvation. When more of the bamboo forests survived, the bears were able to travel to new feeding grounds, but today the giant pandas live in isolated pockets of forest and have nowhere else to go.

In late summer, a female giant panda gives birth to her cubs in a den, which she makes in a hollow tree, rock crevice, or cave. The cubs are helpless when born, and almost hairless. Even though a giant panda may give birth to two cubs, she can only properly care for one. If a second cub is born, it is abandoned and soon dies. For the first month of its life, the mother holds the cub constantly.

Like a human mother, a giant panda cradles her newborn cub as it nurses.

Giant panda cubs soon grow fur to keep them warm, so that they can live through the cold winter. Giant pandas spend most of the time on the ground, but climb trees when threatened.

In 1958, the giant panda was chosen as the symbol of the World Wildlife Fund (WWF), which campaigns to save wildlife. The giant panda is now protected in several reserves in China, but it is still in danger from poachers, who hunt giant pandas for their skins even though the poachers risk the death penalty if they are caught.

27

Bears and People

Throughout history, people have hunted bears for their meat and their fur, and because they were dangerous animals which threatened people's lives and livestock. More recently, the greatest threat to bears has been the loss of their habitats. The human population has more than tripled this century, so more and more land has been needed for housing, industry, farming, and forestry. Today, no kind of bear is common, and some, like the giant panda and spectacled bear, are very rare.

Bears can be trained to walk on their back legs and perform tricks. For hundreds of years, bear owners wandered the cities of Europe making money from their performing animals. Owners often were cruel to their bears, and performing bears were banned in western Europe at the beginning of this century. In some places in eastern Europe and Asia they still perform.

People still hunt bears. Bearskin is used to make clothing or rugs, or can be sold as a valuable trophy. A hunter looking for a young bear to train may kill the mother, not only to keep her from defending her cub, but so that the hunter can sell her fur.

The more we know about bears, the better we should be able to protect them. Until quite recently, very little was known about them. Bears live alone, in places that are hard to reach, so they are difficult animals for people to observe. But scientists have now learned several ways to study them.

To examine a wild bear closely, scientists first shoot it with a tranquilizer dart. While it is unconscious, they weigh and measure it. Sometimes they remove a small tooth, called a premolar, from which they can find out the bear's age.

Scientists sometimes fit a bear with a radio collar, which has a transmitter inside it. They can then track the bear from the signal given out by the transmitter, which can be picked up by a radio. Using this method, scientists have discovered how far polar bears travel in search of food.

The greatest threat to the survival of bears is the destruction or disruption of their habitats. If bears are to survive, we must be prepared to preserve the places where they live.

Bear Review

Giant panda

The giant panda is the bear most in danger of becoming extinct. Fewer than 1,100 survive.

Spectacled bear

No one knows how many spectacled bears still live in the Andes mountains. There are probably several thousand, but their numbers are declining from hunting and from loss of their forest habitat.

Asiatic black bear

Asiatic black bears are declining in numbers from loss of their habitat and because they are killed for parts of their bodies. People will pay a large amount of money for bear paws, which are considered a delicacy, and for gall bladders, which are used as medicine.

American black bear

About 500,000 black bears live in America—more than the worldwide populations of the other seven bears added together. The black bears are carefully managed by North American game services. The numbers killed each year by hunters are controlled so that the population will not fall or rise too much.

Sun bear

The sun bear may be declining in numbers faster than any other bear. This is because its Asian tropical rainforest homes are being destroyed very fast. The bears will probably disappear from some areas before we even know they lived there.

Sloth bear

Sloth bears are increasingly competing with people for land in India. About 10,000 survive, mainly in parks and reserves where they are protected.

Brown bear

It is estimated that there are about 180,000 brown bears; more than half of these live in Russia. In many areas, especially Europe, brown bears survive only in a few isolated places.

Polar bear

In 1973, Russia, Canada, Denmark (which governs Greenland), and the USA agreed to pass laws to protect polar bears, whose numbers were rapidly declining because of hunting. As a result, the number of polar bears is estimated to have increased in the past ten years from 10,000 to 25,000.

MAKING MASKS

VIVIEN FRANK & DEBORAH JAFFÉ

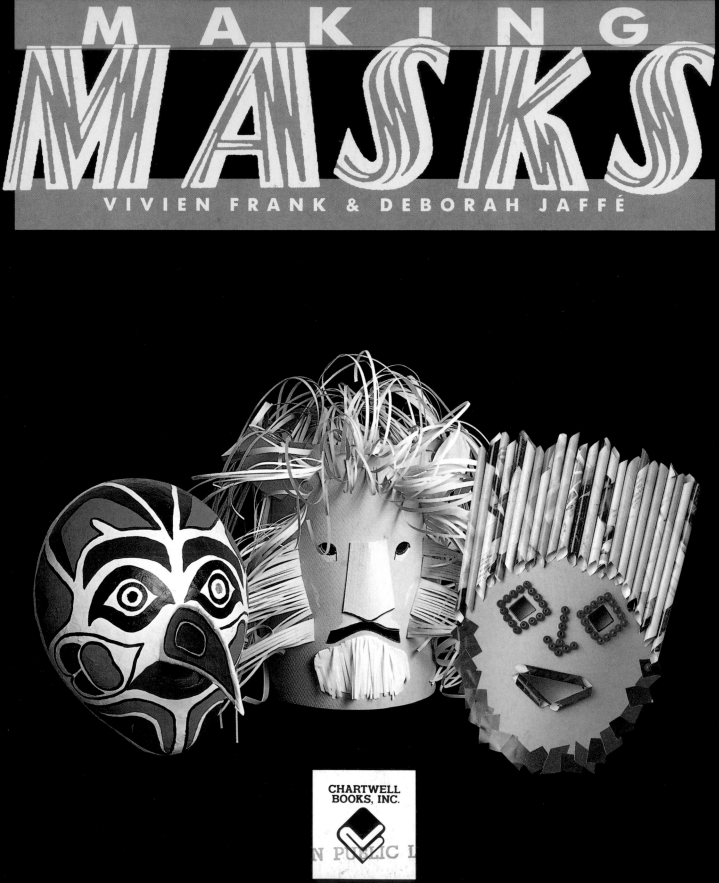

MAKING MASKS

VIVIEN FRANK & DEBORAH JAFFÉ

CHARTWELL
BOOKS, INC.

A QUINTET BOOK

Published by Chartwell Books
A Division of Book Sales, Inc.
110 Enterprise Avenue
Secaucus, New Jersey 07094

This edition produced for sale in the U.S.A., its
territories and dependencies only.

ISBN 1-55521-780-X

This book was designed and produced by
Quintet Publishing Limited
6 Blundell Street
London N7 9BH

Creative Director: Richard Dewing
Designer: James Lawrence
Project Editors: Judith Simons/William Hemsley
Photographer: Ian Howes

Typeset in Great Britain by
Central Southern Typesetters, Eastbourne
Manufactured in Singapore by Eray Scan Pte. Ltd

Printed in Singapore by Star Standard Industries Pte. Ltd.

CONTENTS

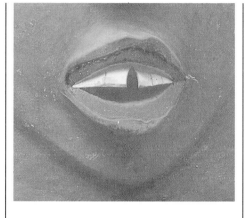

INTRODUCTION

To don a mask is to change character. We all wear invisible masks at different times in our lives for specific situations – the brave face to cope with a difficult situation and the happy face for celebrations. Donning a mask allows the wearer to hide and to say and do things he or she might not normally do. A mask can also be protection, because abuse or attack is directed at the personality of the mask, not the wearer. Like a ventriloquist's dummy, the wearer gives a mask life.

Achieving anonymity by wearing a mask is simple, for even the smallest concealment – covering an eye or the mouth – changes a person's appearance. Bandits, pirates and robbers have used eye patches, eye masks, and mouth masks, as well as knitted face masks, to alter their appearance and avoid recognition.

For thousands of years different cultures throughout the world have made masks for celebrations, to ward off evil spirits, to commemorate seasonal events, for religious and pagan rituals, for dance, and for self-defense. The forces of evil, power, and love have all been symbolized as masks.

Often made from found, local materials, masks have been carefully crafted and sculpted to become beautiful and fantastic objects.

Most children find wearing masks great fun, loving to surprise and scare, while believing themselves to be hidden. Children can also make masks with enthusiasm, beginning with a simple eye mask or paper bag mask and progressing to more complex papier-mâché masks when older. Their designs can be innovative and highly imaginative as they create a favorite animal, TV personality, monster, or dragon.

Members of theater groups, as well as party planners intent on masked or

African antelope skin masks were produced by gifted craftsmen following ancient traditions.

Each mask of the Commedia dell'Arte represents one of the standard group of characters.

Wooden masks from Africa display striking and often intricate carving (above).

costume parties, will find this book packed full of ideas. Although its intention is to give readers an introduction to mask making, with projects carefully laid out in stages, it is possible for enthusiasts to develop their own masks based on learned skills.

As much as they are fascinating, masks are historically and culturally interesting; a brief introduction to the history of masks follows, outlining their significance over the centuries. The main section of the book gives clear instructions on how to make many different types of masks, along with hints on how to wear and adapt them. A list of important mask collections in museums is provided at the end of the book, along with a list of retailers of mask–making materials. A useful bibliography is included for those who would like to delve deeper into this compelling folk–art form.

Masks are great fun to make and wear. We hope you have as much fun creating your own masks from this book as we have had creating the projects and ideas.

South East Asian masks using eye holes (top) and slits below the eyes (bottom).

HISTORY

The cave paintings at Lascaux in France, done by Stone Age people, showing hunters wearing masks of the animals they hunted, are among the earliest records we have of masks. By wearing the mask, a hunter could take on the spirit of the animal and enact the scene he hoped to bring about. Some hunting tribes in parts of Africa and Alaska still perform such rituals.

In ancient Greece and Rome masks were important for physical protection as well as in the theater. Between 700 and 675 BC the Greeks had well-armed and trained armies, equipped with a range of helmets with protective masks. The best of these was a bronze Corinthian type – a metal helmet with side pieces to cover the cheeks and sides of the face and with a long nose piece down the middle. The Roman army, intent on expansion, was also well-equipped, with helmets which had masks for protection and masks for parade. Around AD 200 these were worn by the cavalry for special displays, and some of the masks had female features, thought to have been worn by soldiers disguised as Amazons. Roman gladiators, protected by similar helmets and masks, performed for over 650 years throughout the Roman Empire. By 100 BC they were performing in public to huge audiences, commanding big prizes and much fame.

In the first and second centuries AD, ancient Egyptians made wonderful portrait masks out of plaster, which covered the faces of their dead. The plaster was hollowed out and placed on the face and fastened with cords at the base of the neck. Eyes were painted in on the mask, and around AD 200 false glass eyes were fitted. As Christianity spread, the use of burial masks ceased.

Protective masks have come a long way since the days of Anglo Saxon suits of armor. In the 1600s Italian

hunters had intricate and quite beautiful metal face masks. This century, gas masks and the visors attached to the headgear of baseball players, football players, and policemen are all for self protection. In many cities around the world, cyclists are wearing masks to protect themselves from inhaling too many fumes.

Masks are often employed to ward off evil spirits and Satan. The use of

Italian leather masks are shaped by beating the leather onto a mould.

An Italian rider's mask from about the sixteenth century. It protected the face from branches in wooded country.

dragons and the devil in their craftwork and imagery is very important. In China and South East Asia the dragon mask is integral to the New Year celebrations and in dances to ward off evil spirits. In Bali, the Hindu dance of the Ramayana is cast with actors all wearing different masks to portray the powers of good and evil.

South East Asian dragon masks (below and right) are important in many festivals and are beautiful objects in themselves.

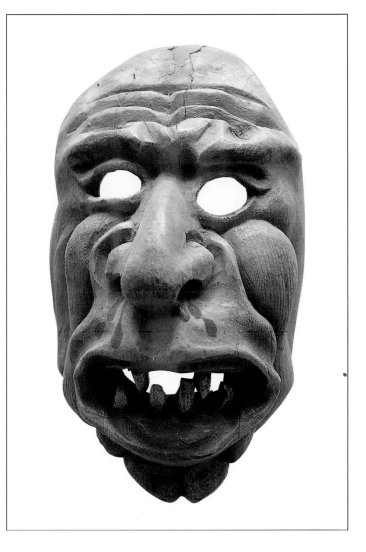

A Roman mask made of pewter, which may have been used by a priest or priestess during ceremonies.

In Austria and Switzerland tree trunks, old hats, and fabric are fashioned as grotesque masks to ward off the winter spirits and welcome the spring and good weather for the crops.

The influence of Catholicism in many countries has been amalgamated with the indigenous culture to create very colorful and witty masks for carnival. The original word, "carnevale," means farewell (*vale*) to meat (*carne*) in Latin. The eating of meat was forbidden during Lent, and the week preceding it was a time for lots of fun and indulgence. Wherever there is carnival there are masks.

The Venetian carnival inspired *Commdia dell 'Arte*, a theatrical style originating in the sixteenth century. The cast wears half masks, enabling the audience to see the expressions of their mouths. The masks are made from all kinds of materials including leather, straw, and fabric. The characters always include a Pierrot, Harlequin,

Punch, the Four Seasons, Sun, and Moon.

The week before Lent is also carnival time in New Orleans, where Mardi Gras, or Fat Tuesday, is celebrated on a grand scale. The streets are filled with floats, and all kinds of masked characters appear, reflecting the different ethnic groups in the city – French Mardi Gras, Black Mardi Gras, and Cajun Mardi Gras. It is thought that Mardi Gras was celebrated in Paris in the Middle Ages and transported to the New World at a very early stage. On March 3, 1699, the French explorer Iberville set up a camp on the Mississippi, south of New Orleans, and called it Point du Mardi Gras. New Orleans itself was founded in 1718, and under French rule, masked balls were held in the period before Lent. The Spanish later put an end to the tradition, but when New Orleans became an American city, the Creole population demanded its

A highly grotesque Austrian mask, carved from wood and painted, which was used at Alpine festivals.

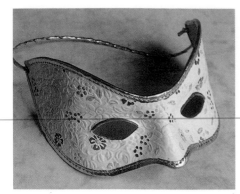

*Masks used at the Venetian carnival are part of a
tradition reaching back to the sixteenth century.*

reintroduction, and in 1827 masks were
allowed in the streets once again. Full
street carnival developed from this
time.

Pre-Lenten carnival is very
important in Trinidad and Tobago and
in Brazil, particularly Rio, where
masks form an integral part of huge
and very ornate costumes. In Britain,
the Caribbean community in the
Notting Hill area of west London
holds a carnival each year at the end of
August lasting three days. This is a
huge event attracting hundreds of
thousands of people.

Many African masks are finely carved from wood and take the form of stylized faces.

In Africa masks are made from antelope skin, straw, and wood. They are beautiful examples of craftwork taking a long time to make. The Yoruba in Nigeria believe a mask can be as simple as a piece of cloth to cover the face or as complicated as a full face, carefully carved, wooden mask. In Zaire, hats with fabric hanging from the brim in front of the face are masks.

In the nineteenth century there was a large mask-making tradition among the Inuit of North America. These masks were left bare and the grain of the wood used to accentuate facial features. Feathers were used to give movement, and paint was used sparingly. Each mask had terrific presence and beauty, reflecting great imagination and skill on the part of its creator.

ranged from partial and whole face masks to masks covering the entire body. They had a fantastic range of expressions, and many were asymmetrical, where the eyes might not be level, while others were half animal and half man. Some looked like birds and mythical creatures.

The basic mask was made of driftwood, sculpted and decorated with an array of found materials – twigs and sticks, feathers, string, and bone all used to great effect. Some

The Inuit used masks for religious and secular activities. The masks were made to symbolize good and bad mythological beings in the creation of the world, the destroyers of that world, gods, spirits, the sun and moon. Essential to the mask's function was the shaman who wore the mask and in a trance state made it come to life. Sometimes the shaman made his, or in some cases her, own masks, although usually they were made by specialist mask makers. This tradition of mask making and carving is still alive today.

Tribes throughout Africa, as well as the North American Indians, the Australian Aborigines, and the New Zealand Maoris have traditionally decorated their faces and bodies with paint and tattoos. These forms of decoration could be called masks – they are used for a number of reasons, including attraction, initiation into a particular group or tribe, fertility rites, and initiation ceremonies.

In the Lancashire and Yorkshire area of England, mummers appear each New Year's Eve. Groups of children and adults dress up, the males as females and the females as males, and cover their faces with black paint. Each has a sweeping brush and does not speak but makes a humming sound. They go from house to house sweeping out the old year, making their humming sound. The best mummers enter the house from the front and leave by the back door, leaving the house free of spirits. Their disguise is so perfect the householders have no idea who they really are.

The application of make-up to the face transforms many women, making them feel more attractive and confident. But it could be argued that make-up is just another form of masking, since it hides the person underneath. Men grow a variety of mustaches and beards which all change the face, sometimes almost beyond

In a modern production of the ancient Greek play The Oresteia *the actors are all wearing masks.*

recognition, and can be used as a very effective form of disguise.

The famous wear dark glasses to make themselves anonymous. Indeed ordinary glasses can alter a person's face, making it look sophisticated and powerful, stupid or intelligent. Glasses are not worn just for opthalmic reasons – Groucho Marx, Dame Edna Everidge, and Elton John would not be the same characters without their idiosyncratic glasses.

Masks and disguise must include the Halloween witch. Although much has been written about the wrongs done against women thought to be witches, she still remains a mysterious character. Beneath the black conical hat her wizened face, pointed nose, blackened and decayed teeth, and straggling hair are fantastic material for the mask maker.

The surgeon's mask protects patients undergoing surgery, at the same time giving him special status and mystery. The bride and widow wear veils to hide their faces. The bride's veil makes her more seductive and denotes virginity, while the widow's veil gives privacy in her sorrow.

The actor's mask has a very old history. Ancient Greeks were the first to use masks for performance. The narrator would use different masks to represent the various characters, and each mask would indicate who was speaking. The word "hypocrite" derives from the Greek word "hyporites" meaning actor; because he often wore a mask he was therefore two-faced.

Noh theater in Japan dates back to the twelfth century. Each Noh mask, in its simplicity, shows a different spirit. The plays deal with the spiritual, the supernatural, demons, and ghosts and are still performed today.

People as diverse as Shakespeare and Walt Disney have made use of the power of the mask, from Bottom in *A Midsummer Night's Dream* wearing an ass's head to Mickey Mouse, made up of a complicated full head mask – and everything in between. Modern actors on both film and stage use a vast array of masks using diverse materials from traditional make-up and human-hair wigs to the latest plastics technology. Mask making is a tradition, and its history continues to evolve.

A plain modern manufactured mask can act as a canvas onto which an infinite variety of characters and expressions can be painted.

TECHNIQUES

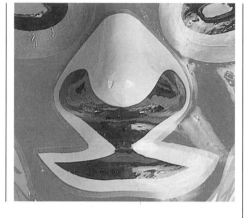

The masks in this book are to a great extent suitable for most people to wear. In a few cases the masks have been specially designed to suit children or adults, and this fact has been noted in the instructions, but in general the masks can be adapted to accommodate various sizes.

If you have never made a mask before it would be wise to start with one of the simpler styles at the

beginning of the project section. However it is quite unnecessary to work through all the methods in the technique section before starting on a mask. This section is intended to operate as a reference area for the various ways of creating masks.

The template section, starting on page 112, has most of the templates and patterns for the masks in the book. Some of these are shown full-size and some will need to be enlarged; this is explained, and information is also given on ways of altering sizes.

There are some general rules about faces which apply to everyone. Look at the diagram on this page and you will see that the eyes are situated approximately halfway between the top of the head and the chin. In young children the eyes are a little lower. You will notice that the bottom of the nose lies halfway between the eyes and the chin, with the mouth coming halfway between nose and chin. The ears fit between the eyes and the bottom of the nose.

Positioning eye holes in the mask is one of the most important and difficult things to do. They should not be made too large, because too much of the wearer's own eyes would show and this might detract from the effect of the mask. On the other hand, if they are too small the wearer will be unable to see properly. In some masks, notably in Mexico and South America, the eye holes of the masks are slits cut into the mask at a place to suit the wearer but bear no relation to the design of the mask, which is elaborately decorated. One way of minimizing the effect caused by large eye holes is to make a feature of them by sticking net across the space. This will enable the wearer to see quite clearly but will completely shield the eyes and expression from the audience.

Gloriously coloured paints characterize many South East Asian masks.

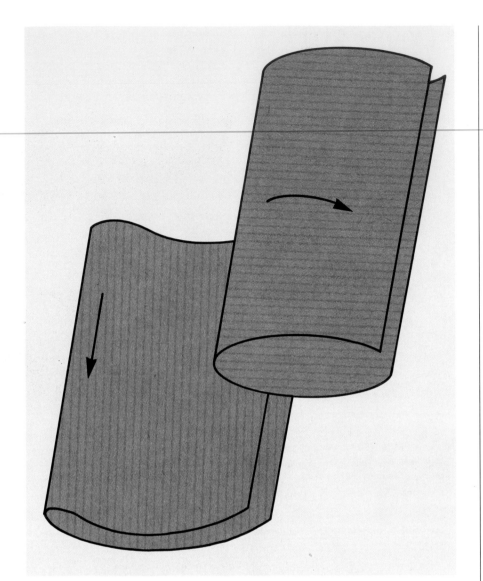

bottom. It will bend more easily in the direction of the grain – see diagram. Stiff paper or board should be held in the middle of the sides and flexed. Then turn the sheet 90 degrees and repeat. As with paper, the board will flex more easily in the direction of the grain. In the project section of the book you will sometimes find that one of the dimensions of the paper measurements is underlined. This has been done in cases where it is important that the grain run correctly.

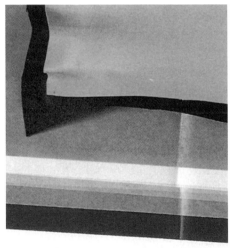

PAPER PROPERTIES

Many of the masks in this book have been made from paper of various kinds, and several have been decorated with paper. It is well worthwhile spending some time in a good art-supplies store, becoming acquainted with the different kinds of paper that are available and that you might use. In addition to familiar papers such as drawing paper and tracing paper, you will find several different weights of colored paper, ranging from tissue and decorative Japanese papers to stiff mat board (used mainly in picture framing), with medium-weight colored papers in between. You will also find illustration board, which is a stiff white board that comes in several weights and can be used for many of the projects in this book.

On imported European papers you may find a number followed by gsm or g/m^2; this means "grams per square meter" and is a useful guide to the weight (or thickness and density) of the paper. For example, 150 gsm indicates a light-weight paper; 150 to 230 gsm is medium-weight; stiff paper and boards will have a higher gsm number.

It is important to understand that all papers have a grain running in a particular direction. This direction should be ascertained in order to use the material to advantage.

To find out which direction the grain runs in any piece of paper, lay the sheet on a flat surface. Bend the paper over on itself from the side and press gently with the hand. Repeat this action, bending the paper from top to

SAFETY

Some masks go right over the head – paper bag and fur fabric masks, for example. These are relatively loose and allow for easy breathing, but *never* use any form of plastic bag for mask making.

DECORATIVE TECHNIQUES

Cutting

Paper and board can be cut with a craft knife, but the surface on which you are cutting must be protected either with a cutting mat or, if that is not available, scrap cardboard or old newspapers.

Paper can also be cut with scissors, but remember to keep separate scissors for paper and fabric. If you are cutting a curve, try to move the paper around as the scissors are closing but held in the same position. This will insure a smooth curve. For a decorative effect pinking shears can be used.

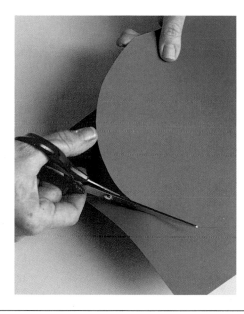

Tearing

This technique is suitable for any weight of paper. It is useful to know the grain direction when tearing paper, because a smoother edge will result if the paper is torn in the same direction as the grain. It is also possible to control the tear. When torn against the grain, the paper will have a more jagged edge.

DECORATIVE TECHNIQUES

Punching

This is an easy and effective way of decorating paper or board. It can be done with big or small holes. There are several types of hole punch available, including the single hole punch bought at a stationery store, the revolving head hole punch normally associated with leather work, and the type used in conjunction with rivets (if using this type, make sure the work surface is protected). Draw faint pencil lines and try to punch the holes evenly.

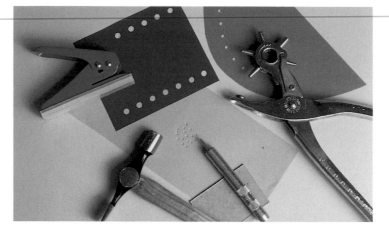

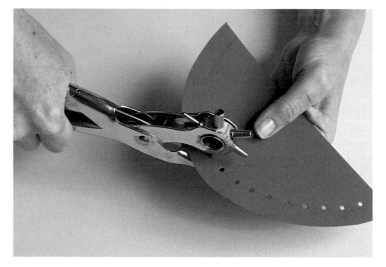

Scoring

This technique is very useful and will help give a professional finish to many projects, as a scored line will bend more easily. The purpose of scoring is to open up one side of the paper by drawing a line with a blunt point. This can be the scissor points or the back of a cutting knife, but care should be taken not to cut through the paper. Sometimes, with thick board such as that used for the horse's head mask (see page 105), it is necessary to cut through half of the thickness of the board and bend away from the cut. It would be wise to practice this on a scrap of the board being used for the project. There is a tool called a bone folder, used in bookbinding and leatherwork, which can be used for scoring.

DECORATIVE TECHNIQUES

Pleating

This is another way of using paper for decorative purposes. The folds will crease more crisply if they are made with the grain, where possible. If accuracy is required, the position of the folds can be measured prior to folding, and scoring the lines will make the process of creasing easier.

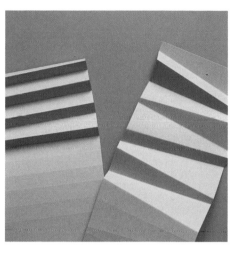

Rolling

Paper can be rolled around various objects and held in place with some form of adhesive, depending on the final use of the roll. Rolls can vary from pencil size to large cylinders. As with the previous method the roll will be best achieved if created with the grain. This applies especially in the case of whole head mask, such as the lion's head (see page 102).

Curling

To make paper curls, cut the paper against the grain and then pull the strips, one by one, across the back of a knife, scissor blade, or ruler – this causes the paper to stretch on one side and thus curl. Practice with different weights of paper to discover what works best for your purpose.

Scrunching

This is a fun method but is best suited to very light-weight papers. Cut or tear the paper into squares or triangles and screw up the pieces. This can be done tightly or loosely, and the resulting shape can be glued in position where required – sometimes a little glue may be added to the shape.

FASTENINGS AND FIXINGS

There are numerous ways of attaching pieces of paper, board, and fabric together. Some of these ways are listed here, but you will probably think of other methods. Some of the methods are suitable only as a temporary measure, but they are still important, particularly when an extra pair of hands is unavailable!

Tapes

There are three main types of tape used in mask making: masking tape, which has low tack and is extremely useful for temporary fixing and usually does not mark the material that is being held; transparent tape, which is usually sold under a brand name; and double-sided transparent tape, which is excellent for creating invisible bonding.

Glues

There are many types of glue available, and each person has his or her own favorite brand. In this book we have used mainly white, all-purpose glue. This glue is clean to use, dries transparent and allows the user time to position the parts being attached. Sometimes a quick-drying glue is required, and for this purpose a clear glue such as household cement is suggested.

Staples

These are very useful for joining parts together quickly, but make sure to cover the open ends with tape if they are anywhere near the face.

Paper clips

Extremely handy for holding various parts together temporarily.

Paper fasteners

These can also be used in a temporary or permanent way, but remember that quite a large hole is required in which to insert the fastener prior to opening out the parts. The advantage of this type of fixing is that it allows movement of the parts attached.

Again, it would be wise to tape over the open ends of the fasteners if they are to be used for any length of time.

Needle and thread

Sometimes a needle and thread may be the easiest way of joining two parts. This may be particularly appropriate when attaching two dissimilar materials, such as fabric to cardboard. The thread used must be strong enough to support whatever is being attached, so choose a thread that will not break easily, such as button thread.

SAFETY

At all times be aware of safety factors. Make sure that children are always under supervision.

When using craft knives and hole punches always work on a surface which is protected with a cutting mat or thick scrap card.

Never pierce the eye holes when the mask is in front of the face or over the head. Always mark the eye positions with a pencil and then remove the mask from the head before cutting the holes.

Slots and tabs

These are methods of creating fixings without using any other material. A slot is cut into one piece of material and a tab is added to the other piece of material. This tab is then pushed through the slot. Sometimes glue or tape can also be used to create a more permanent fixing. If the board is thick, it may be necessary to enlarge the slot slightly to accommodate the tab.

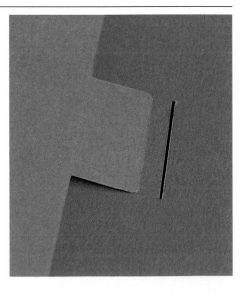

METHODS OF FIXING MASKS

There are several ways of fixing masks so that they can be worn comfortably. Sometimes the type of mask dictates the method of fixing, as with the Rider mask (see page 75), but as a general rule, the best way to choose a method is to experiment with all the ways of fixing and select which one suits you the best.

Elastic, string, or ribbon attached to the mask at about the level of the eyes is the easiest and most common way of fixing the mask.

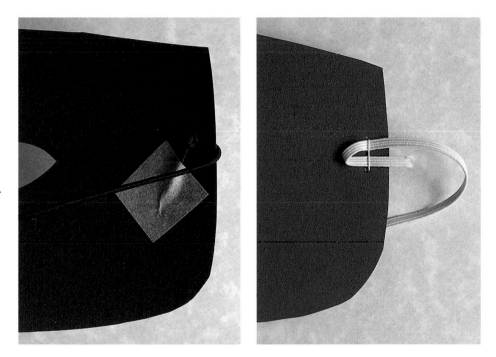

Method 1 – Elastic

If fixing the elastic by piercing a hole and tying, always strengthen the area of the mask where the hole has been made so that the weakness caused by the hole is reduced. This can be done by sticking masking tape over the hole area on the inside of the mask, so that the decoration of the mask is unaffected. Alternatively, staple the elastic in position and cover the staples with layers of tape for the wearer's protection.

The most suitable and comfortable type of elastic to use is hat/military/round cord elastic, but thin, flat elastic can be used if this type is not available.

Two rubber bands looped through the holes in the mask and stretched around the ears can be used as an impromptu fixing, although this may not be comfortable to wear for a long period of time.

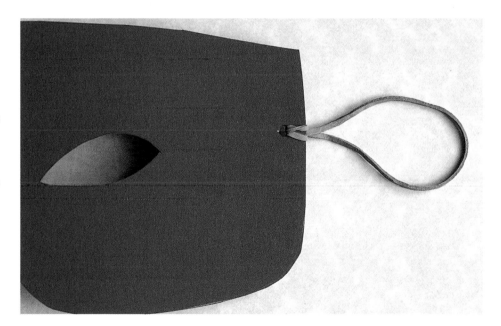

TIP
If there are places where a mask rubs the face or otherwise feels uncomfortable, it is quite easy to glue a piece of soft material, such as stockinette, to the inside of the mask using glue or tape.

METHODS OF FIXING MASKS

Method 2 – String

If you decide to use string, make sure that the knot securing the string to the inside of the mask is larger than the hole, or use staples. In either case stick a piece of tape over the ends to keep them in place. The string can be painted to match or contrast either with the hair of the wearer or with the design of the mask.

Method 3 – Ribbon

Thin black cotton ribbon was traditionally used in Victorian masks, but more exotic ribbons can be used as part of the decorative effect of a mask, for example in the Masked ball mask (see page 48). The ribbon can be held in place with staples, but make sure the ends are covered with tape so that they do not scratch the face.

Method 4 – Sticks

This is a useful way of fixing a mask when it does not need to be kept permanently in front of the face. There are two ways of using sticks.

Style A If the mask is a flat whole face mask, such as the Dragon mask (see page 82), a flat piece of wood can be attached to the center of the chin of the mask. The stick should be stuck in place with glue and the glued end covered with tape. This method is good for young children.

Style B If the mask is an eye/domino mask, such as the Masked ball mask (see page 48), a small round stick is normally used. This can be fixed with glue and/or tape to the side of the mask or slotted through two holes (see diagram). The stick can be painted or decorated to suit the mask.

In both cases the length of the stick will depend upon the person carrying the mask, but it is wisest to make the stick too long and cut it down to size as required.

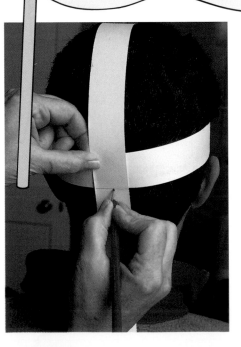

Method 5

When making an oversize mask, such as the Dragon mask on page 82, a different method is required. A quick and easy way is created by using strips made from stiff paper.

Take a strip of stiff paper about 1in/2cm wide, and fix this around the head of the person who will be wearing the mask; secure this ring with tape.

Next fix another strip at right angles to the ring, and place the ring back on the head. The second strip should be at the center back.

Bring the loose end over the crown of the head, and fix it at the front so that it sits comfortably. This headgear, when firmly taped, can be fixed to the centre of an oversize mask and will be most comfortable to wear.

PARTIAL MASKS USING ACCESSORIES

SCARF

A scarf is an important part of disguise and mask making. It can be wound around the head and face in numerous ways. For the Yoruba in Nigeria a mask can be as simple as a piece of cloth covering the whole head and face. A pirate might wear a scarf over his mouth and nose.

The type of fabric, its color, and its pattern all change a scarf disguise. A piece of plain black cloth implies something sinister, whereas a piece of thin voile in a delicate color and print means something magical and fairylike.

● 1yd/1m square of black net covering the head and face.

● One black scarf covering the mouth and nose and another covering the head, with only the eyes visible.

● Red dotted handkerchief over the mouth, fastened at the back, giving the look of a bandit.

GLITZY GLASSES

Eyeglasses and sunglasses can form the basis of an eye mask. With suitable glue and paints they can be quickly transformed, and when combined with a mustache, colored teeth, and a plastic nose, they can make movable masks.

MATERIALS

- old eyeglasses or sunglasses
- glue suitable for plastics
- sequins
- long pin or matchstick

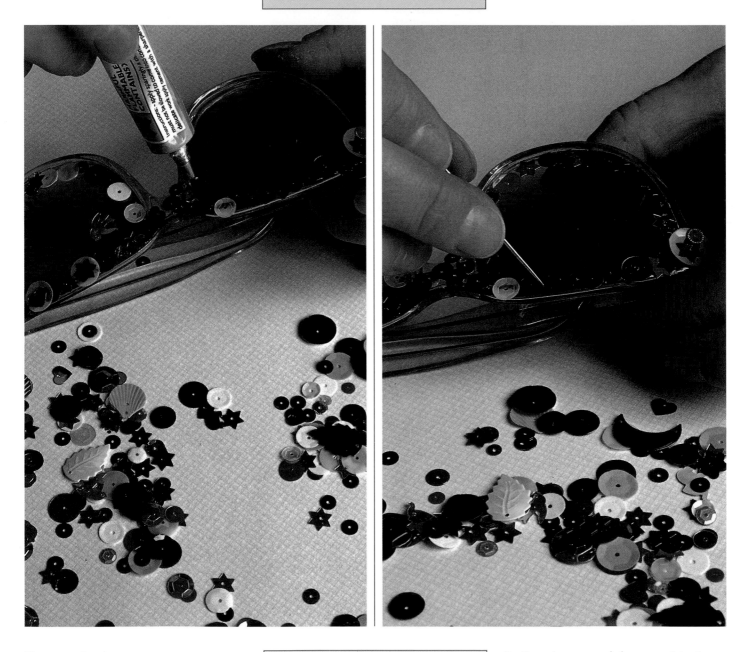

Preparation

1. Make sure the lenses are clean. Carefully put a thin layer of glue around the top of the frames and stick sequins on it, using a pin or matchstick to help put them in place. Put a little more glue on top of the sequins. Stick more sequins onto this to build up a thick layer.

TIP

Try making "Funny Eyeglasses" by painting the shape of an eye with white enamel paint on the dark lenses and gluing false eyelashes around them.

2. Put glue around the rest of the lens, up to the frame. Stick on sequins. Glue a single sequin on the lens. Leave the glasses to dry.

ORANGE-SKIN TEETH

This is a very old-fashioned type of disguise which looks striking, gruesome, and amusing at the same time. It is particularly useful at Halloween. Peel the orange carefully. If possible do this by dividing the orange skin into six segments. Lay one of the pieces, orange side upward, on the cutting mat and slice through the center, leaving ½in/1cm uncut at each end. Now cut jagged teeth on either side of the slit. Place the orange skin in your mouth between lips and teeth and look to see whether you like the result. You have five other possible sets on which to practice or to make for your friends.

PAPER FRAME EYEGLASSES

Another eyeglasses disguise can be achieved by making frames from mat or illustration board and decorating them in whatever style appeals to you — this could be severe and heavy-looking, or it could be stylish and extravagant.

Many different decorative materials can be used; the only limitation is your imagination. The exotic styles shown here are simply extensions of the basic shape. You will find all three templates on page 113, and you could experiment with the basic shape yourself to create your own styles.

Preparation

1. Trace the pattern from the templates and draw it on the mat board. If you are using foil-faced board, draw on the wrong side. Cut out the frames.

2. If you are using the shorter piece of board it will be necessary to fix the bows with tape. This should be done before decorating so that the tape can be hidden as much as possible – decoration can be glued over the tape.

3. Now begins the fun of decorating. The basic shape has been adorned with strung sequins, as they can be glued in curls and twists quite easily.

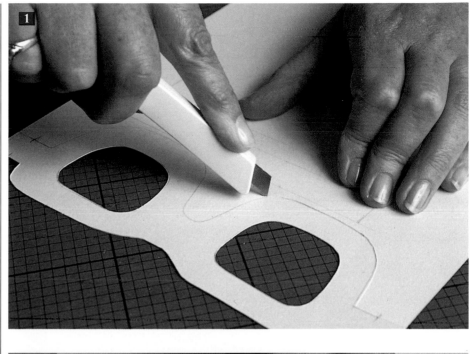

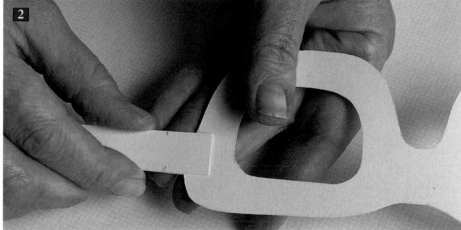

MATERIALS

- eyeglasses template, page 113

- pencil

- tracing paper

- stiff mat board for the basic shapes 17in × 5in/42cm × 13cm, or 7½in × 4in/18cm × 10cm

- craft knife

- glitter pens, sequins, feathers, net, tissue paper, pipe cleaners, etc.

- clear glue and tape

● The spiky shape looks extremely glamorous, made here with foil-faced board, 11in × 5½in/28cm × 14cm. The mask could be lavishly decorated with fake jewels, or various other colors of foil-faced board could be glued on.

● The butterfly glasses are cut from board measuring 7½in × 5in/18cm × 12cm. They have been decorated with glitter paints, strung sequins, and loose sequins. Adding net "lenses" enhances the delicate style. A harmonizing pipe-cleaner has been pushed through the middle of the top and twisted so that it stays in place.

FACE PAINTING

Decorating and painting the face makes a mask. Throughout the world different cultures have used this method as part of their mask making. North American Indians painted beautiful patterns on their faces, and in parts of Africa tattooing and face painting are still practiced.

MATERIALS

■ a range of face paints and crayons

■ old lipsticks and rouge

■ cleansing cream

■ absorbent cotton

■ cotton swabs

■ headband or scarf to fasten hair away from the face

The use of face paints and make-up is very important in the theater. The simple application of eye make-up and lipstick to accentuate an actress's features can make her look more beautiful or ugly, younger or older. A skilled make-up artist can paint lifelike wounds and scars, wrinkles, and beauty spots on a face.

The clown uses face painting to change his face completely, enlarging his mouth and lips, drawing shapes around his eyes or on his cheeks to create a face that immediately tells us he is a clown. A mime artist tries to minimize the face by covering it in white face paint, adding just a little detail, usually in black, around the eyes. This minimalist effect allows him to use his face to express any emotion he wants, being happy or sad depending on the way he uses his mask.

TIPS

■ Use only face paints, face crayons, and make-up, *never* ordinary paint. Have cotton and face cleanser on hand to clean the face afterward.

■ You might want to combine face painting with a partial mask. An eye mask for a ball, for example, might require painted lips and a beauty spot.

■ The winter eye mask (see page 50) could be worn on a frozen face – painted white and pale blue.

■ The full face dragon's head (see page 82) might need a painted nose and lips.

■ A witch (see page 64) combines many mask components – hat and nose, for example – and requires good, dark, spooky make-up to make her come alive.

DUAL FACE

You can paint the two halves of the face in whatever color you wish, making sure they are strong enough in contrast to be noticeable. Draw a thin line in the darker of the two colors down the middle of the face. Fill in the lighter half of the face first, then the darker half. Accentuate the eyes, and outline the mouth with a thin black line, or apply dark lipstick to the lips.

Preparation

● Before applying make-up or face paint, decide on the character you want to create and study a picture of the face and its features carefully. Either copy one of the designs given here or create your own, but practice first on the outline drawing of the face.

● After you have selected your character you can start on the real face. Tie your hair back in a headband or scarf, and make sure your face is clean. Apply the foundation or base color first. Some characters will not need this as the bare flesh will be the base color.

● Accentuate the eyes.

● You may want to paint in other features on the face.

● Do your mouth last.

● Look at the face and make any minor adjustments.

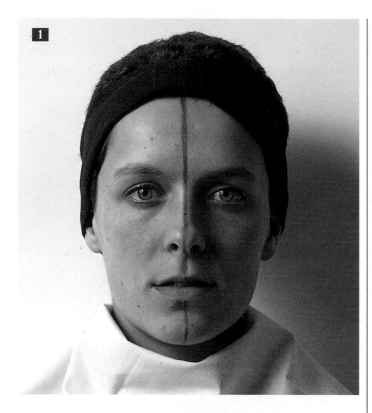

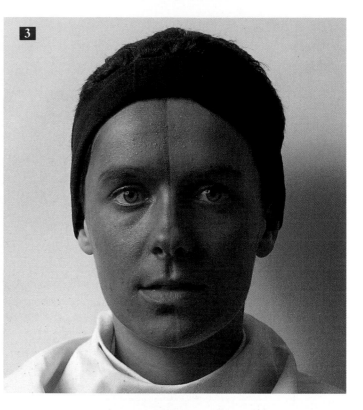

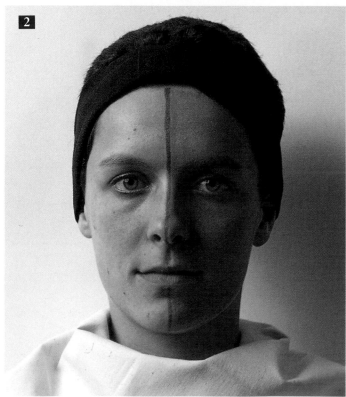

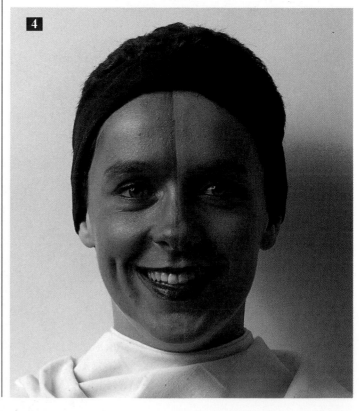

BEAUTY

Leave skin flesh color, or apply a little foundation. Accentuate eyebrows. Apply eyeshadow and shape the eyes with thin black lines. Use false eyelashes, or paint in eyelashes in black on lower lid. Put rouge and a beauty spot on the cheeks. Accentuate the lips with red glossy lipstick.

CAT

Look at the face carefully and work out where the stripes will go. Select your base color. White is a good base color, and ginger, brown, and gray are good for stripes. Draw in lines for the stripes, fill in pale areas, including the lips, and then dark areas. Paint in a small rectangle on the tip of the nose. Draw in the whiskers in black; or you could add paper whiskers.

PIERROT

Draw in the shapes with a thin black line. Fill in the white area, then the shapes in black. Paint the lips black.

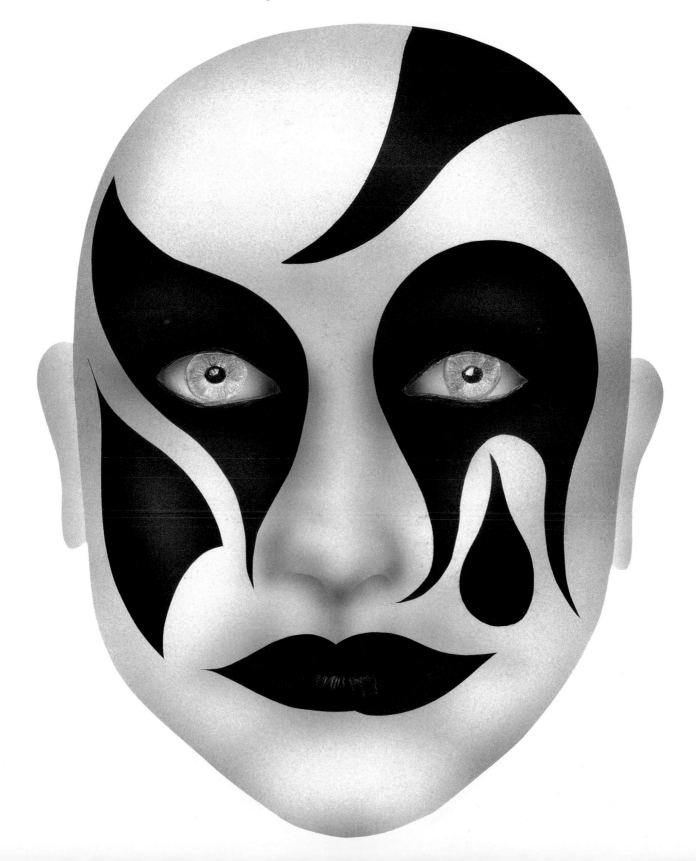

CLOWN
NUMBER 1

Leave skin flesh color or cover with white. Draw the outlines of the shapes around the eyes and fill in. Accentuate the eyes by drawing thin black lines around them. Paint a large red circle on the end of the nose. Draw in the lips.

CLOWN
NUMBER 2

A different clown's face, more angular and austere, but still filled with life and laughter. The steps for producing this face are shown opposite.

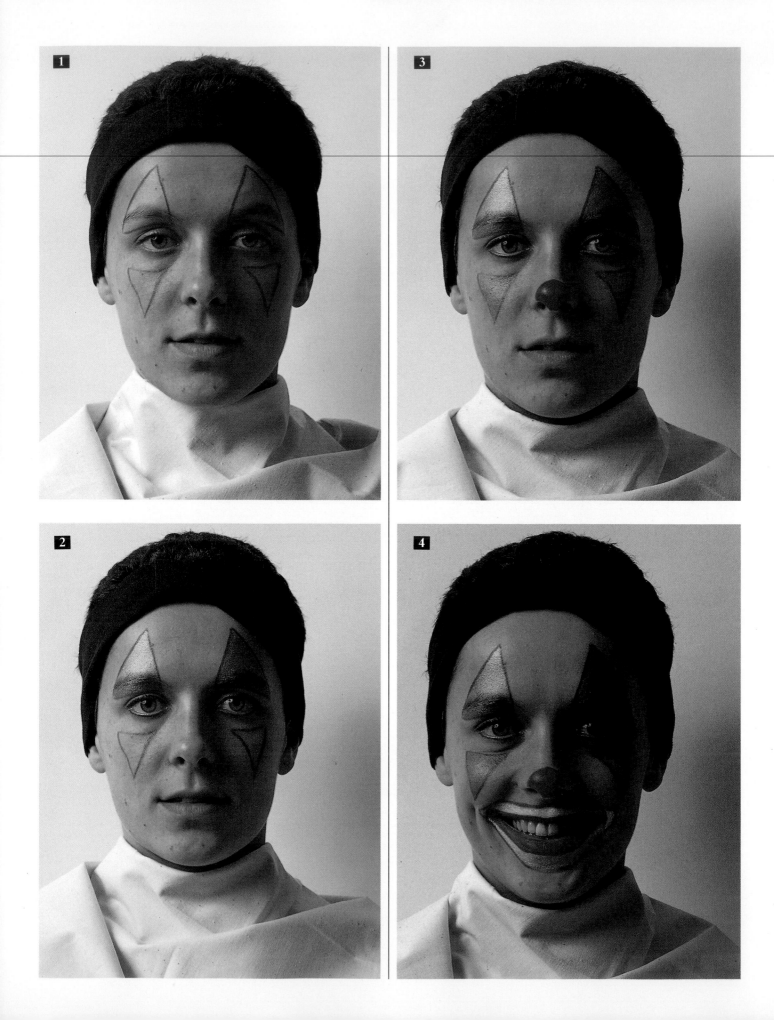

EYE PATCH

The first requisite of any pirate is an eye patch. It makes him look more powerful and mysterious. Although people have to wear eye patches as a result of injury or illness, for some reason an eye patch does seem to convey status and mystery. For example, Moshe Dayan, the famous Israeli statesman in the 1960s and 1970s, always wore a black eye patch. He was instantly recognizable and seemed confident and mysterious.

Preparation

1. Using white chalk, draw around the eye patch template on stiff paper or felt. **2.** Cut out the shape.

MATERIALS

■ eye patch template (see page 114)

■ stiff black paper or black felt

■ white chalk or fabric-marking pencil

■ hat elastic or narrow black ribbon

■ needle and black thread

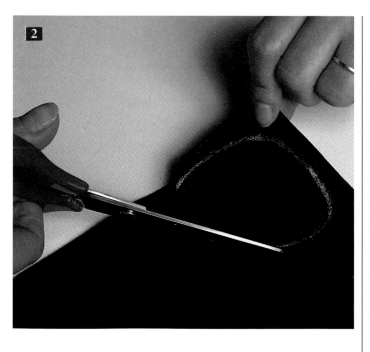

3. Make holes for the elastic. Pass the elastic through, knotting it at both ends on the back of the patch. If you are using felt, you might like to sew two pieces of ribbon to the back of the patch, where the punched holes for the elastic would be (see techniques section, page 20).

PARTIAL MASKS

Burglar Bill

Burglar Bill is the archetypal thief. He can wear this black eye mask on its own or combine it with a knitted face-mask (see page 96), a scarf (see page 24), or an old flat cap.

Preparation

1. Decide whether the mask is to be made out of mat board or felt. Trace around the template with pencil on the board, or with white chalk on the felt.

2. Cut out mask using scissors or a craft knife (see techniques section page 16). Cut out the eye holes also.

3. For the fastening use method 3 (see page 19). You might decide to sew black flat elastic to the sides of the mask in line with the eye holes.

MATERIALS

- eye mask template number 1

- light-weight black mat board 10in × 4in/25cm × 10cm or black felt the same size

- white chalk

- pencil

- scissors

- craft knife

TIP

Since this is a basic mask, you could cut it out of white or colored board and decorate it with fiber-tip pens and paint for a different character.

MASKED BALL

A masked ball is great fun. We are never quite sure who is underneath the mask. You can cover this mask with sequins or scrunched paper or a mixture of both decorations.

MATERIALS

- eye mask template (page 115)

- metallic foil-faced mat board 10in × 4in/25cm × 10cm

- sequins

- scrunched tissue paper

- all-purpose glue

- pencil

- craft knife and scissors

Preparation

1. Draw around the template on the board, and cut out the mask. Cut out the eye holes. Put a thin layer of PVA glue around one of the eye holes and cover with sequins.

2. Put a little more glue on top of this and some more sequins. When all is dry, put a thin layer of glue on any loose sequins. The glue is colorless when it dries.

3. Either repeat step 2, above, on the other eye hole, or dip the bottom of scrunched pieces of paper in glue and stick them around the eye hole.

Use method 3 for fixing, or, if you want to add more excitement to the mask, attach a stick to the back of the mask using method 4b.

TIP

There are many decorative variations of this mask; you could use small colored buttons or beads instead of sequins. Curl bits of chenille yarn around a pencil, and glue them to the top of the mask to make antennae.

THE FOUR SEASONS

The portrayal of the seasons is very important in the Venetian Commedia
dell 'Arte, *as well as in the various medieval books of days. By using a
mixture of natural and artificial materials you can make a series of very rich
seasonal eye masks.*

MATERIALS

- eye mask template 3

- all-purpose glue

- craft knife and scissors

- pencil

Spring
- light-weight light yellow or light green mat board 10in × 5in/25cm × 12cm

- small dried or artificial flowers in light colors

- artificial leaves

Summer
- light-weight white illustration board 10in × 5in/25cm × 12cm

- artificial or dried flowers in bright colors

- feather butterfly – optional

Fall
- light-weight white illustration board 10in × 5in/25cm × 12cm

- dried leaves, rosehips

- dried flowers in brown, red, and gold colours

- dried barley, oats, or wheat

- small artificial berries in orange, yellow, and purple.

Winter
- light-weight pale purple or pale blue metallic mat board 10in × 5in/25cm × 12cm

- dried moss

- dried leaves

- white paint and brush

- silver spray paint

Each of the four masks uses the same mask template. Their decoration will depend on the materials you have available. For spring you may have to rely on artificial flower buds, and in summer there may be brightly colored dried flowers available. If it is fall, you may be able to gather crisp leaves, dried flower heads, and rosehips from the garden and barley and oats from a farmer. Winter requires twigs and evergreen shrubbery and some bright berries, which can be artificial.

There are a number of retailers of artificial-flower-making components, and it is great fun to see what you can do with artificial stamens, petals, and leaves. Many craft and gift shops sell dried flowers, and a small bunch, once dismantled, will go a long way in mask making.

Preparation

1. Select the season you are going to make, and draw around the template on the appropriate board. Cut out the eye shapes. Build up the mask gradually. Attach leaves and larger flowers first by dipping them in glue and sticking them onto the mask. Let them overlap the edge of the mask.

2. Put on the smaller bits like buds, small flowers, and fruits last.

Spring is evoked by light, fresh, clean colors.

Deep, rich, vibrant colors represent summer.

Fall is a time of rich mellow, warm colors.

Silver gives a sense of the cold, brittle hardness of winter.

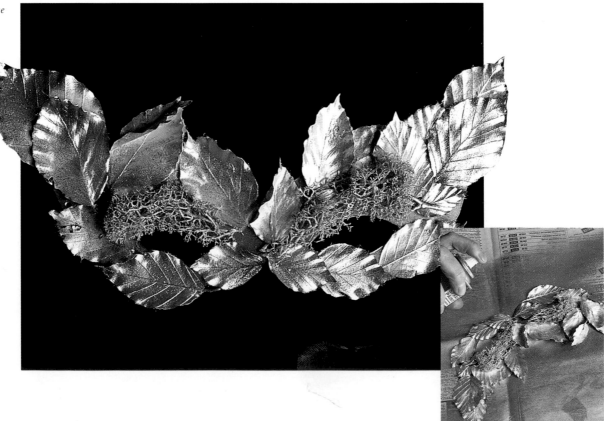

3. Look at your mask carefully to see that it evokes the right season; make any adjustments. Check that you can see through the eye holes, and if necessary trim away any excess foliage. Use method 1 or 4 for fixing.

4. For the winter mask, paint the leaves white before gluing them down, then put moss around them. Leave some of the background bare, and spray the whole thing with a thin layer of silver spray paint.

TIP

You can use this method to make a bird mask by covering the white background with feathers and a few sequins.

EYES AND EARS MASK

The two masks shown here are both made from the same basic pattern, and you will probably think of other animals that can be created from the same template. Both cat and mouse can be made from a variety of colored papers, or the background could be painted to create a tabby effect. The important thing to remember is that you are trying to represent the essentials of the animal – a mouse has large ears with pink inside; a black cat often has green eyes, and cats generally have pointed ears.

Preparation

1. Trace the patterns from the single template on page 116. Draw the pattern on appropriate board and cut out carefully, trying to make the curves as smooth as you possibly can.

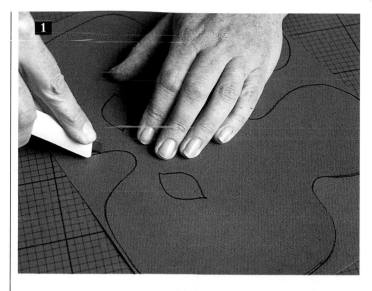

2. Cut out the ear linings from the colored paper.

3. Glue the ear linings in place, centering them on the ears.

MATERIALS

▪ animal template, page 116

▪ pencil, scissors, and craft knife

▪ tracing paper

▪ light-weight mat board in gray and black 11¾in × 8¼in/ 29cm × 21cm

▪ scraps of pink, pale gray, and green paper

▪ glue

▪ elastic or ribbon

4. Cut out eye holes, using the craft knife on a protected surface.

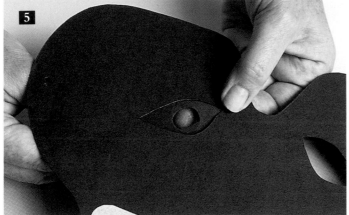

5. For the cat, cut scraps of green paper to be glued behind the eye hole, and cut a much smaller hole in the center of each piece. Make holes on the sides of the mask for the elastic, and tie it to fit.

HARLEQUIN MASK

This style of mask can be made to look very spectacular, offering ample opportunity for lavish use of decorative materials. In this example a variety of papers have been used, including foil and fluorescent, patterned, and colored paper. In addition, pieces of leather and fabric have been introduced – a marvelous way of using leftovers from other projects. Traditionally the Harlequin is dressed in patchwork, and this is why the costume is made up of different-colored squares.

Preparation

1. Trace the pattern from the template section, and enlarge using the grid system explained in that chapter. Draw the pattern on the wrong side of the board, and cut out very carefully.

If you are using foil-faced board for the basic shape, it will be necessary to cut the face area from some plain white board first, then glue the foil in position on the main shape. The dotted lines on the template indicate this area. If you are using plain white board you will only need to mark this area.

2. A diamond grid with the shapes 1½in/4cm apart has been used in this example, but this is quite arbitrary, and other designs or measurements can be substituted. First mark your chosen design on the right side of the board. Then cut up lots of pieces of decorative materials so that they will fit within the grid and arrange them.

3. When sticking the shapes in place, continue right to the edges. Cut away the excess areas from the wrong side when you have finished.

MATERIALS

- Harlequin template, page 118

- pencil and ruler

- scissors and craft knife

- tracing paper

- mat board for mask, about 20in × 20in/50cm × 50cm

- clear glue and tape

- materials for decorating

- strips of stiff paper 1in/2cm wide for head fixing

4. To give a neat appearance, braid or other materials may be stuck over the joins between the shapes.

5. When the decoration is finished, the nose piece can be fixed in place. First score along the line marked on the pattern, and then curve the nose gently and glue it in place on the rear side of the face piece.

6. Glue the face piece in position on the mask.

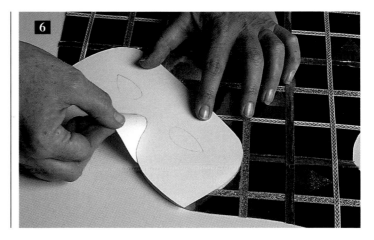

7. Now cut out the eye holes. Finally, make the head fixing, following the instructions on page 19.

CROWNS AND CORONETS

Kings, queens, and princesses are incomplete without crowns and coronets. This simple mask can be lavishly decorated to become a crown or more simply made into a coronet (as shown here) for a young princess. You could have a royal family celebration.

MATERIALS

- crowns and coronets template (see page 117)

- stiff white paper 9in × 6in/ 23cm × 15cm

- stiff metallic paper in gold, silver, or bronze 13in × 7in/ 33cm × 20cm

- craft knife

- hole punch

- tape

- double-sided tape

- glue

- sequins, sequin strips, beads, jewels, colored papers

- paints and paint brush

- thin ribbon for mask fastening

- soft white net or silver foil film for a veil (optional)

Preparation

1. Draw around coronet part of the template on the wrong side of the metallic stiff paper and cut it out. Draw around face piece on white stiff paper, and cut it out. Then cut out the eyes. Try on this part of the mask, and make any necessary adjustments to the nose and cheek areas. Paint in the facial details. The princess should be delicate and feminine. (See face painting, p32.)

2. Cut thin pieces of sequin strip about 3in/8cm long to make a fringe. (You could use paper strips for this, even curling some of them. See techniques section page 16.) Put double-sided tape along the top of the face part, and carefully lay the sequin strip on this.

3. The coronet can be decorated in many different ways. Treat each segment in a uniform way. The princess will need simple decoration, some silver-sprayed flowers (use small silk flowers or flower-making components), plastic pearl beads, and some filigree along the edges.

4. When you have finished decorating, lay the coronet over the face part, then, making sure it is in position, gently press it down. The double-sided tape should hold it in place while you turn it over and tape it firmly on the back. Attach some ribbon to the back of the mask for the fastening (see techniques section, page 19).

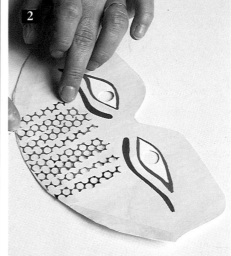

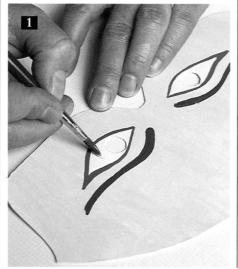

● If you want to make the princess more magical and fairy-like you could give her a veil. Real bridal net is very expensive but you could use cheap dress net. The quantity will depend on the size of the princess and how long you want the veil. Lay the net on top of the head and let it hang down the sides and back. Put the mask on, and fasten it over the net.

● Give a king strong, bold eyebrows and eyes. You might want to put a few wrinkles around his eyes or give him a mustache using face paints. On his crown use big plastic gems, or glue on cut pieces of colored foil giftwrap and scrunched tissue paper, sprayed gold and silver.

● To make an Ice Maiden, drape silver foil film over the head, like the net, and place a silver or blue metallic coronet over it.

HALLOWEEN HAT

The Halloween hat shown here can be personalized in many ways and can also be adapted for other purposes. Some of the ideas shown in other chapters could be used in conjunction with the hat.

Preparation

1. The hat is made in two parts – first the crown, which is cone-shaped, and then the brim. Lay the sheet of black paper on a flat surface. Attach a piece of string to the pencil, and make a mark on the string 18in/45cm from the point of the pencil. Place this mark in the corner of the paper and hold firmly. Position the point of the pencil on the edge of the paper so that the string is taut. Keeping the string under tension, draw an arc to the other edge.

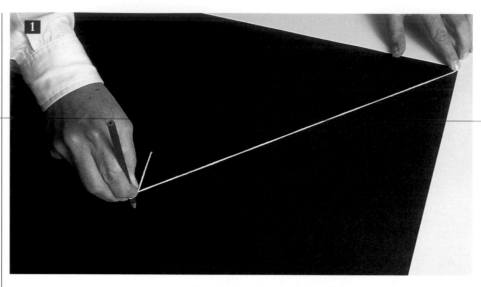

2. Cut out this shape, which is a quarter circle.

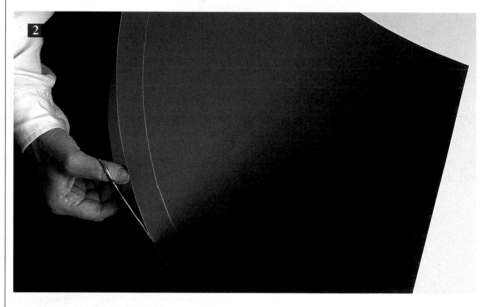

MATERIALS

- pencil and string

- scissors

- medium-weight black paper about 33in × 24in/85cm × 60cm

- clear glue and tape

- green and black crepe paper

3. Now cut slits along the curved edge 1in/2cm deep. These will be used to stick the cone to the brim. Bend these tabs to the outside. Next curl the paper around on itself to form a cone. In order to make a neat finish, cut out a small square at the top. Since heads vary in size, before the cone is fixed permanently, try it on, so that any adjustments can be made. The cone should be glued, and then a little tape can be stuck inside for extra security.

TIPS

- An average head measures about 24in/60cm, and a child's head a little less. In order that a child should not be dwarfed by the hat, mark the string at 16in/40cm and make the brim a little narrower.

- If the paper is too floppy for the brim, two circles can be cut at step 4 and the second can be glued to the underside of the hat, after the tabs have been glued in place.

- This hat could be made in mat board of any color and be used in conjunction with the hat masks; see page 98.

4. To make the brim, stand the cone in the middle of the remains of the sheet of black paper, with the tabs turned to the inside, and draw around the edge. Next decide on the width of the brim – 4in/10cm is average, but it could be more or less, depending on the wearer and weight of the paper. The wider the brim, the heavier the paper will need to be, so that it does not flop down and hide the face. Draw a line the chosen width away from the first circle. Cut on both pencil lines, and you will be left with a ring of paper.

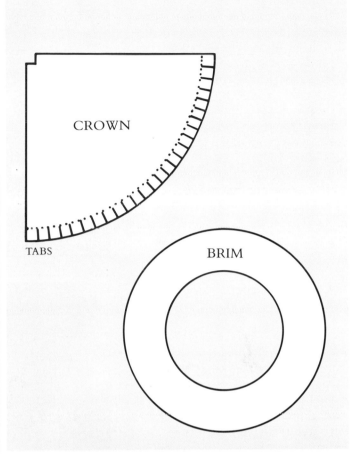

CROWN

TABS

BRIM

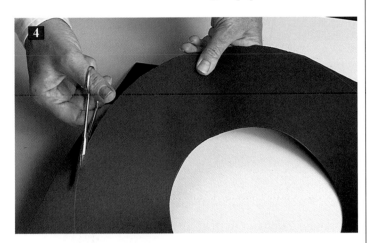

5. Push the cone through the hole in the center of the brim so that the tabs, cut in step 2, are on the underside of the brim. Check that everything fits neatly, and then, using the glue, stick the tabs in place on the brim.

6. To make the character more gruesome, you can add hair to the inside of the hat by cutting strips of the crepe paper and taping them inside the cone. Cut off a piece of each of the green and black crepe paper which will fit around half of the hat and is at least 16in/40cm long. Fold both pieces in half, and put the black piece inside the green piece. Leaving a solid area of 1in/2cm at the top, cut narrow strips to represent hair, and stick in place, using double-sided tape.

PAPIER-MÂCHÉ NOSE

This is a very simple shape to create, and once you have made one, you will probably want to experiment with lots of different shapes and sizes. A nose can be used on its own or with many different masks, as well as with a witch's hat.

1. Create the basic shape of a nose using thick paper or card. You will probably need one piece for the bridge and one for the bottom of the nose. Join the pieces with masking tape.

2. Tear some newspaper into small pieces and dip them into the diluted glue (see instructions for papier-mâché on page 89). Cover the nose shape evenly with several layers of newspaper. Try to make the final layer very smooth, covering the edges. Leave to dry thoroughly. If necessary sand any rough edges with fine sandpaper, then paint with white water-based paint.

MATERIALS

- pencil and scissors
- tracing paper
- medium-weight card
- masking tape
- old newspapers
- PVA adhesive
- white emulsion paint
- brush and paint
- elastic

3. Having decided what kind of character the nose should represent, paint it to suit. When finished it could be varnished for durability. Hold the nose in place, and decide where to make the holes for the elastic. Pierce carefully and thread the elastic through the holes and tie the knots.

FULL FACE MASKS

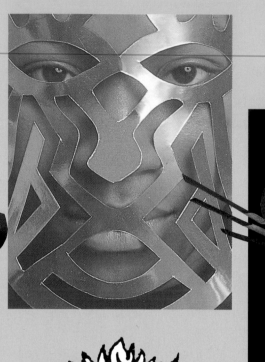

FULL FACE PAPER MASKS

A paper mask is the easiest full face mask to make. The simple shape can form the basis of numerous masks, and it is not difficult to build up three dimensions from the flat surface.

ZEBRA

The template can be scaled up or down to fit the size of the wearer's head. Make it somewhat larger than the actual face, as it will curve slightly when it is fastened.

MATERIALS

- basic face mask template, page 119

- light-weight white illustration same size as template

- pencil

- craft knife

- black paint and thin brush

- black and white paper

- glue

Preparation

1. Draw around the template on the board; and cut out the shape. Cut out the eyes, nose, and mouth. Draw in the zebra's stripes, in pencil, making them about ⅓in/1cm wide. Paint a thin black line around the eyes, nose, and mouth. Paint in the stripes and leave to dry.

2. Make paper curls ¼–½in/5–10mm wide in black and white paper (see techniques section, page 16).

3. Stick them to the top of the head. Use methods 1, 2, or 3 for fixing (see techniques section, page 19).

MOUNTAIN MASK

Tibetan masks are a great source of inspiration for the following mask, which should be very subtle in color and materials.

MATERIALS

- basic face mask template page 119

- light weight dark green or dark blue mat board same size as template

- 14 white shirt buttons

- strip of maribou feathers – 15in/38cm long

- 10 oval compressed paper shapes

- gold or bronze paint

- all-purpose glue

- craft knife

- scissors

2. Paint the paper shapes gold or bronze, and when they are dry, glue them above the eyes to make eyebrows.

3. Cut the feather strip into 2 pieces, one 12in/30cm long and the other 3in/8cm long. Glue the shorter piece around the top of the head and the longer one around the bottom and sides of the face. Use method 1, 2, or 3 for fixing (see techniques section, page 19).

Preparation

1. Draw around the template on the board, and cut out the shape. Cut out the eyes and mouth. Glue the buttons around the eyes.

FANTASY FULL FACE MASK

Preparation

1. Draw around the template on the board, and cut out the shape. Cut out the mouth. Change the eyes into diamonds, drawing the shapes first, then cutting them out. Outline the eyes in black fiber-tip pen, and glue the beads around them, about ¼in/5mm from the edge.

2. Glue a line of 6 beads vertically, between the eyes for the nose, and make a "v" shape of beads at the bottom for the nostrils.

3. Take a color page from a magazine, and cut random geometric shapes about ½in × ¾in/1cm × 2cm. Glue these around the bottom part of the mask to make a beard.

MATERIALS

- basic face mask template, page 119

- light-weight yellow ocher card same size as template

- 45 small red wooden beads ¼in/5mm in diameter

- color pages from a magazine

- all-purpose glue

- craft knife

- black fiber-tip pen

- pencil and ruler

4. Make paper rolls (see techniques section, page 16) out of another page.

5. Make the rolls 4in–6in/10cm–15cm long, and glue them across the top.

6. Make three rolls of the same color – one 3in/7cm long and two 1½in/4cm long. Glue these around the mouth. Use method 1, 2, or 3 for fixing (see techniques section, page 19).

RIDER MASK

This mask simulates the sixteenth- and seventeenth-century Italian riders' masks, which were worn to protect the face from branches when riding through wooded countryside. They were cut from thin sheets of metal and formed a type of armor. The designs could be quite decorative, however, and they inspired the simple cut-out mask here.

Preparation

1. Trace the basic mask shape. Either draw your own design or choose one of the rider mask patterns shown. If the mask is for an adult, take it to a photocopy shop and ask them to enlarge the pattern by 20 per cent. Trace the design onto the back of the foil-faced board, and then cut away the shaded areas with a craft knife. Make sure the work surface is protected, with either a cutting mat or some cardboard. Turn the mask over, and smooth the cut edge where the knife may have caused a slight burr. If you are using white board this may not be necessary.

2. If you have made the mask from white board it should now be covered with the aluminum foil. Lay the foil over the mask, and cut roughly to size, allowing enough to turn over the edge. From the wrong side, cut a slit through each open area. Turn right side up, and bend all the edges to the back, making sure no excess shows. Hold the mask up to the face, and mark the position of the holes for the elastic, string, or ribbon. Pierce the holes, thread, and tie.

MATERIALS

■ basic face mask template, page 119

■ paper and pencil

■ silver foil-faced board or white board and aluminum foil 11in × 9in/28cm × 23cm

■ craft knife

■ elastic, string, or ribbon

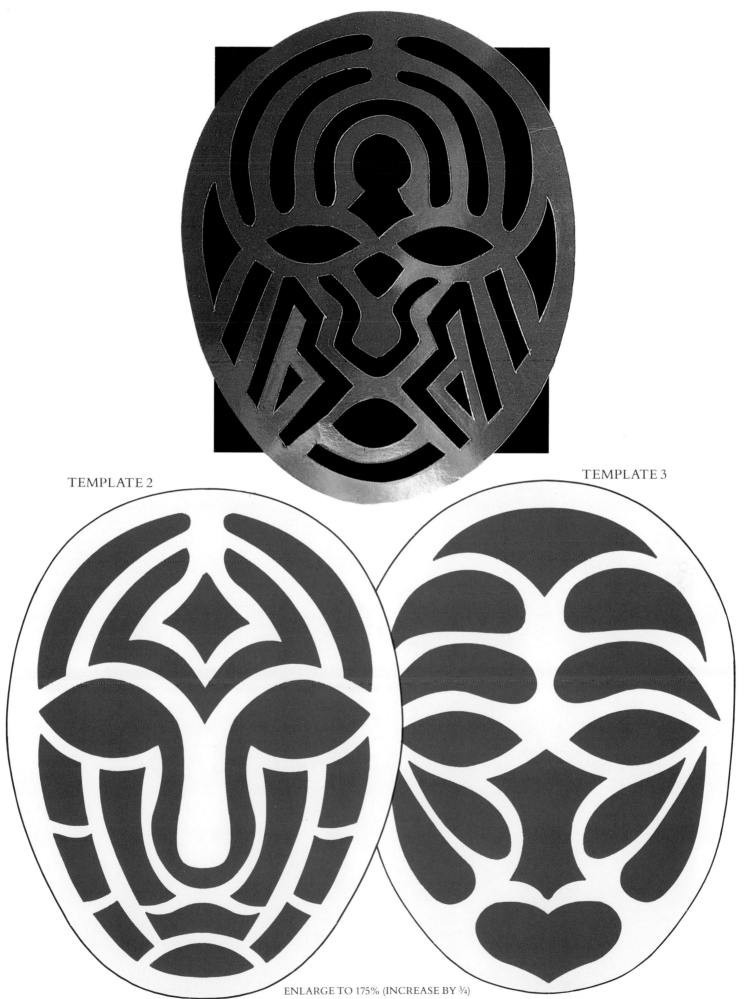

TEMPLATE 2

TEMPLATE 3

ENLARGE TO 175% (INCREASE BY ¾)

ORIGAMI MASK

Quick and easy to make, the origami mask is extremely versatile. It can be made to represent many characters. In this example, the mask is decorated with paints and marker pens. As an alternative, the mask makes a very good bird.

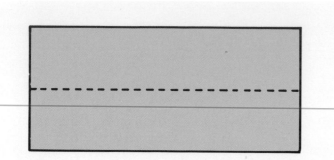

VALLEY FOLD

EXISTING CREASE

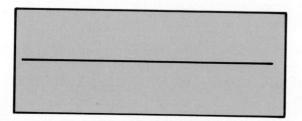

FOLD TOWARDS YOU

FOLD AWAY FROM YOU

MATERIALS

- pencil and ruler

- scissors or knife

- black light-weight paper

- hole punch and string

Preparation

1. Take paper measuring 12in/30cm square for a child or 14in/35cm square for an adult. As with all masks, these measurements are adjustable for the individual. Fold and crease the paper diagonally, and then flatten it before folding the two side corners to the previously creased center line.

TIPS

- It is important to fold origami on a firm, flat surface such as the top of a table.

- If you have not done any origami before, check that you understand the basic symbols shown on this page.

- Always make the fold crisply, but do it slowly to insure that you get the crease exactly where you want it to be.

- It may be a good idea to practice by folding a mask from a small square of paper first, before starting on the mask itself.

2. The paper now looks like this.

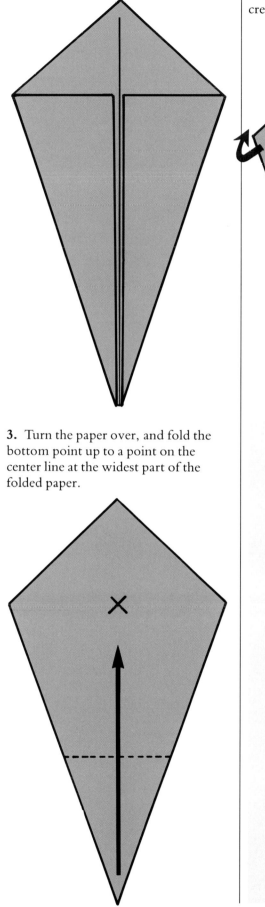

3. Turn the paper over, and fold the bottom point up to a point on the center line at the widest part of the folded paper.

4. Fold the paper (including the point) toward the back along the previously creased center line.

5. Now pull the point forward, and crease at a suitable angle to represent a beak or a nose.

6. Cut out appropriate holes for the eyes, and decorate as you like. Make small holes at the widest point and attach the ties. Fixing methods 1, 2, or 3 would be suitable for this mask.

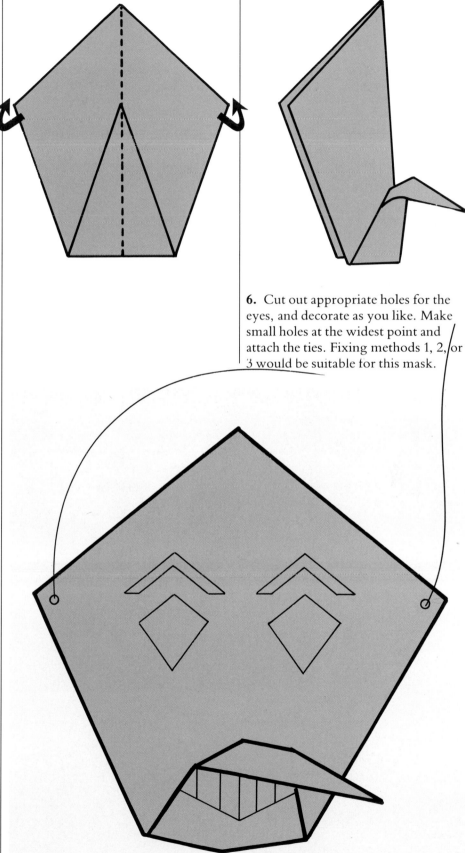

DRAGON

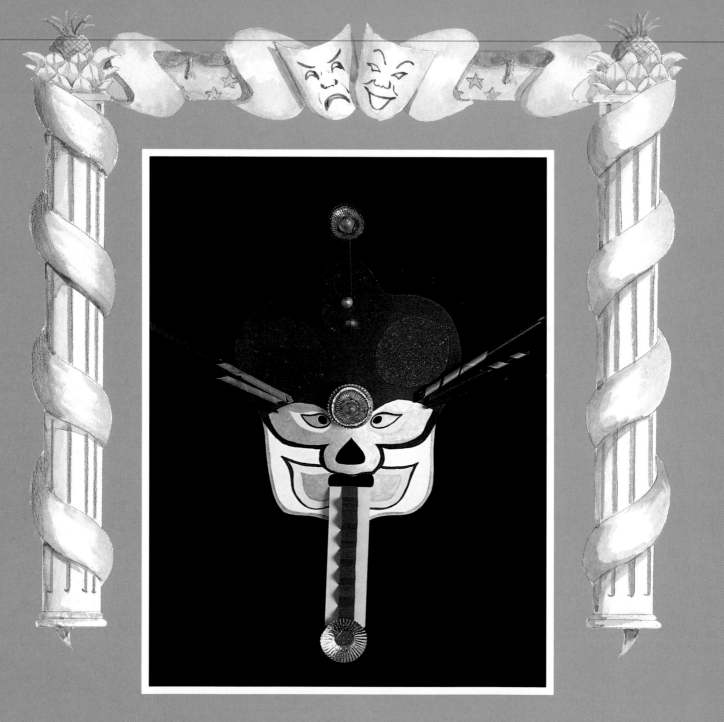

A very important symbol in all parts of Asia, especially China, Hong Kong, Tibet, Sri Lanka and Indonesia, the dragon is a colourful and crucial element in many celebrations and festivals. Often the dragon is made into a large whole-head mask, sometimes with a large mouth, articulated jaws, huge bulbous eyes and a large mane of coloured hair.

This dragon is a flat mask and is very simple to make. It can be as ornate and decorative as you want depending on the materials you have available. The mask can be made to wear on the face or attached to a stick to wave in front of the face when appropriate.

Preparation

1. Draw round the template onto the white card and cut it out. Draw round the head-dress area onto the black or dark coloured paper and cut it out. Stick this shape onto the white card.

2. Draw in the facial features with silver or gold metallic markers. Make the eyes and mouth big and bold.

3. Add the final details of the face with red and black paint.

4. When decorating the head dress stick lots of brightly colored materials onto the black paper area. Do not be afraid of having lots of different colors and textures, but do aim for some symmetry to avoid ending up with a mess. Cut out three bright shapes from the crinkle foil and stick them onto the head-dress.

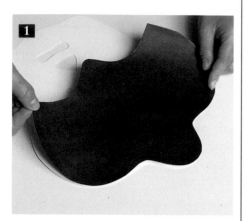

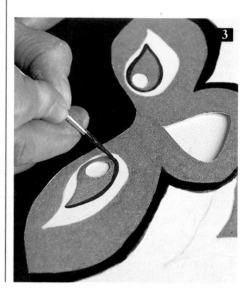

MATERIALS

- dragon template page 120

- medium-weight white card 14in × 12in/35cm × 30cm

- black or dark colored paper 12in × 8in/30cm × 20cm

- colored papers in 2 lengths of contrasting colours 2in × 12in/ 5cm × 30cm

- gold or silver metallic marker

- paints and thin brush

- pulp shapes

- lollipop sticks

- colored translucent paper or tissue paper

- colored crinkle foil paper

- various metallic and coloured fondant cases

- PVA glue

- pencil

- craft knife

5. Add painted or natural lollipop sticks, and stick painted pulp shapes, fondant cases or scrunched tissue paper (see techniques section page 18) onto them. Stick these to the top of the head-dress. Make paper rolls (see techniques section page 18) out of translucent paper or tissue paper and stick these to the sides.

6. Make the tongue by taking a strip of coloured paper 2in × 8in/5cm × 20cm (or longer if you want). Fold over one end and make a point at the other. Take a piece of paper ¾in × 12in/ 2cm × 30cm in a contrasting colour and pleat it, making each pleat about ½in/1½cm side. (See techniques section page 18.) Put a little glue on alternate concertina fold edges and stick it down the middle of the previous long strip of paper.

7. Hook the folded end of the tongue into the dragon's mouth and stick with tape, from behind. Stick a metallic fondant case or other decoration to the bottom of the tongue. This forms a basic tongue but you could always add further decoration to it. For fastening use method 5 or 4A (see techniques section 19).

TIP

■ The wearer's nose could be painted a colour – white or deep red (see face paints section page 32).

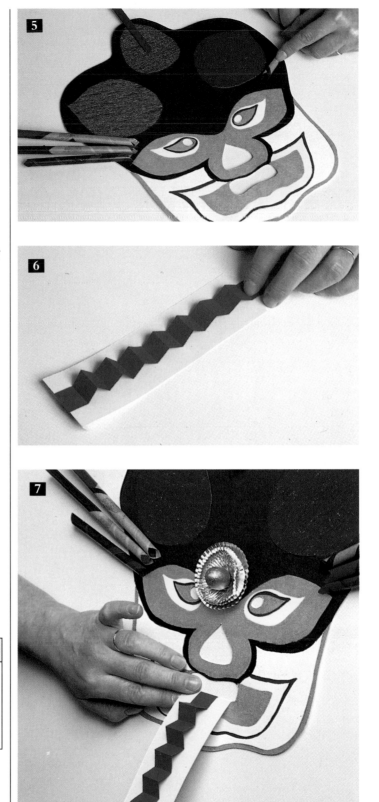

THE SUN AND MOON

*These extended full face masks of the sun and moon are made out of flat
board and complement the Four Seasons masks.*

MOON

Preparation

1. Draw around the template on the board, and cut out the moon shape. Cut out the eyes, nose, and mouth. Draw in the arc to make the crescent. Scrunch (see techniques section, page 16) and tear tissue paper and doilies and glue to the crescent shape of the board to make a rich, but not too thick, textured surface. Try to keep the curve of the crescent arc.

2. Spray the crescent with silver paint.

3. Paint the rest of the mask dark blue/black for the night, and when dry put the star stickers on. Use method 5 for fixing (see techniques section page ▮▮).

MATERIALS

- sun and crescent moon template page 121

- light-weight white illustration board 12in/30cm square

- white paper doilies

- white tissue paper

- silver and gold glitter

- silver spray paint

- dark blue and black paint

- paint brush

- gold and silver star-shaped stickers

- glue

- pencil

- craft knife and scissors

SUN

Preparation

1. Draw around the template on the white board, and cut out the sun shape. Cut out the features as for the moon. Make a collage on the sun's face, as in the moon mask (step 2 in the previous project), using the yellow tissue paper. Outline the smiling eyes and mouth with a thin row of scrunched orange tissue paper. Carefully arrange the yellow tissue paper so that it covers the nose.

2. Gently spray with a thin layer of gold paint, retaining some of the yellow and orange color beneath.

3. Trim around the edge of the face.

MATERIALS

■ sun and crescent moon template page 121

■ light-weight white mat or illustration board 12in/30cm square

■ light-weight white board 8in × 24in/20cm × 60cm

■ gold crinkle foil paper 8in × 24in/20cm × 60cm

■ pale yellow and light orange tissue paper

■ gold spray paint

■ pencil

■ craft knife and scissors

■ glue and tape

4. Cut out the sun rays in white board, three of the smallest shape and six each of the larger shapes. Cover the sun rays with gold crinkle foil paper.

5. Place the smallest three rays at the bottom of the face, and tape from behind. They should slightly overlap and be taped to each other as well as to the mask. Repeat this process around the sun with the other rays, alternating their shapes. By overlapping they will support each other and not flop when in position. Use method 5 for fixing (see techniques section, page 19).

TIP

You could use this sun as a basic shape and paint it with orange, yellow, and gold paints.

AMERICAN INDIAN MASK

This style lends itself very well to the shape created by a papier-mâché balloon mask. Traditionally carved from wood, the mask images are usually taken from animal forms. American Indians lived in harmony with nature, and their folklore gave equality to all living things. Although they recognized that their physical appearances differed from animals, they felt they were descended from them, and each tribe had a special affinity with a particular animal such as a bear, a wolf, or an eagle. It is for this reason that many of their carvings take the appearance of half animal, half man.

Preparation

1. Blow up the balloon so that when it is held in front of you it is impossible to see the face. Tie firmly with string and cover with a thin coating of the release agent. One balloon will make two masks. Dilute the glue with water to the consistency of thin cream, and

MATERIALS
■ light-weight mat board
■ balloon and string
■ release agent (petroleum jelly)
■ old newspapers
■ all-purpose glue
■ tracing paper and card
■ pencil
■ craft knife and scissors
■ sandpaper
■ water-based paint
■ paint brushes
■ paints
■ varnish

tear the newspaper into strips about 1in/3cm wide. Make sure your working area is protected, as the next stage may be a little messy. Cover the balloon with the first layer of paper. If the balloon jumps around a bit, hold it in place on top of a bowl.

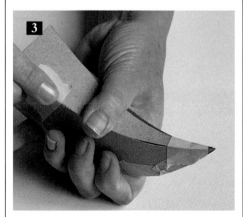

3. Make the beak shape next. Cut two side pieces and one base piece from light-weight board. Glue these pieces together with masking tape and cover with several layers of glue-soaked newspaper strips. It will be necessary to use quite small strips in order to cover the shape smoothly. Leave both balloon and beak to dry for 24 hours.

2. Put on second layer – try to use paper of a different color to make it easier to see what you are doing. Continue in this way until you have completed eight layers. Try to make the last layer especially smooth to save time and work later.

4. Now cut the papier-mâché balloon in half. It is easier if you draw a line around the balloon first and then cut carefully on the line with a craft knife, using a sawing action. The balloon may pop, or it may just stick to the insidfl of the mold but it will peel away easily.

5. Put on some lipstick and place the mask in front of your face. When it feels as if it is sitting comfortably, press your lips to the inside of the mask so that the lipstick marks the position of the mouth. Draw the desired mouth shape on the inside, and cut this out. On your own face, measure up from the mouth to the bridge of the nose, and mark this distance on the mask. Now measure the distance between the centers of your eyes. Mark the position of the eyes on the papier-mâché. Draw in the shape of the eyes and cut them out.

6. Take the beak shape and trim the open edges. Using masking tape, stick the beak in position on the mask. Now take some newspaper strips and diluted glue, and cover the join with two or three layers of paper.

7. Trim the edge of the mask, and then bind all the cut edges – outer, mouth, and eyes – with small pieces of newspaper. Leave to dry again.

8. Next draw the outline of the final design on the surface of the mask. Mix the colored paints to a smooth consistency and paint carefully. Allow the paint to dry overnight, then varnish. Make holes in the sides of the mask slightly above eye level, and thread string or ribbon through the holes so that the mask can be tied in place.

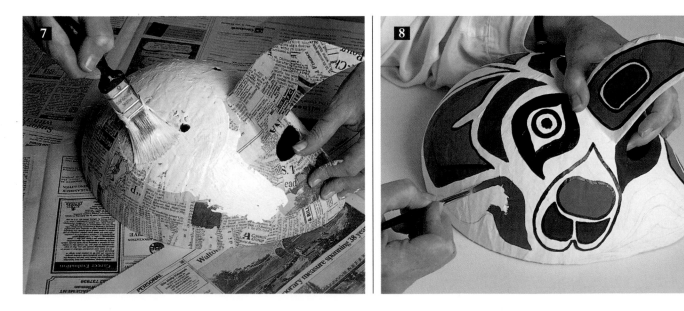

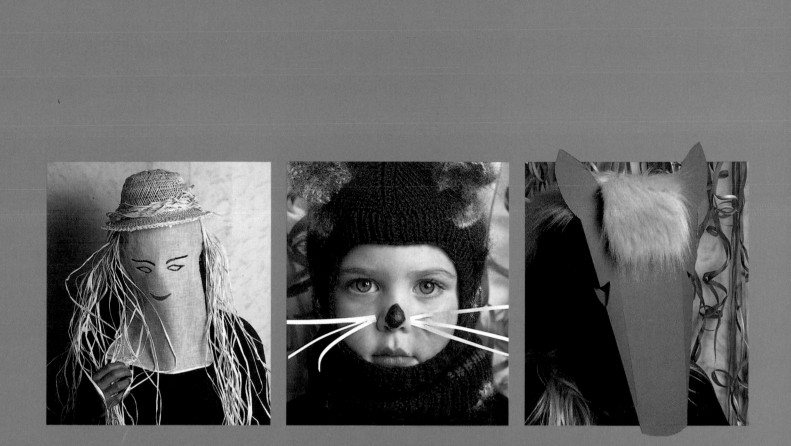

WHOLE HEAD MASKS

BAG PEOPLE

Paper bag people are very easy and quick to make. The more varied your paper bags, the more interesting the crowd will be.

Preparation

1. Try the bag on the head, and make sure it fits. Pull it well down, and carefully pencil in the eyes and mouth positions. Take the bag off and lay it down. Using the basic face template, draw in the shapes of the eyes and mouth over your pencil marks. Put the piece of cardboard inside the bag to make a cutting surface. Cut out the eyes and mouth. Paint in the details of the lips, eyes, and eyebrows; add cheeks and wrinkles if you want, too!

2. Make hair out of lots of thin ribbon, and stick it all over. Alternatively you could make hair out of colored paper cut into fine strips, some curled (see page 16) and some straight and glued on, as for the lion on page 102. Colored tissue and crepe papers can be cut into strips, some with straight edges and others zigzagged with pinking shears. Paper doilies can also be used. A variety of different hairstyles will quickly appear.

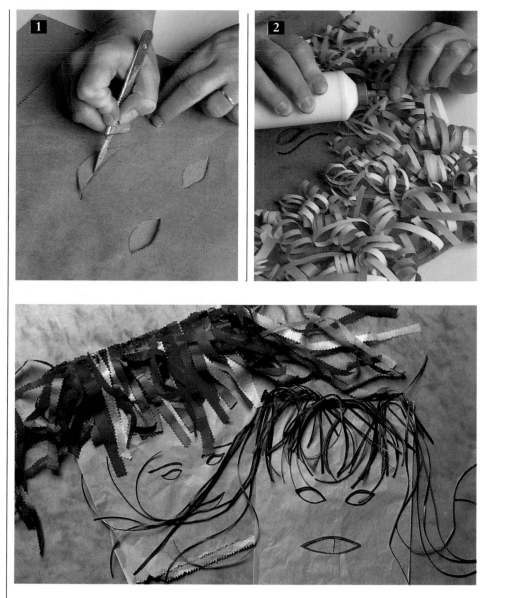

MATERIALS

■ large paper bag about 12in × 16in/30cm × 40cm (check that it fits)

■ basic face template, page 119

■ piece of thick cardboard, slightly smaller than the bag

■ craft knife

■ all-purpose glue

■ red and black paints and brushes

■ decorative materials such as thin ribbon, crepe paper, tissue paper, and colored paper

SAFETY

Use only paper bags, not plastic bags, which are very dangerous because they may cause suffocation. If you have any doubts about the bag you have chosen, do not use it.

KNITTED FACE-MASK

This mask can be used by itself or in conjunction with an eye mask for total anonymity. The knitted face-mask, or "balaclava," originally used by soldiers on active service in the second half of the 19th century, was a woolen covering for the head and shoulders. It was probably designed for purely practical reasons during the Crimean War at the Battle of Balaklava, where the cold was bitter. A similar type of head covering can be seen in the Bayeux Tapestry, where it appears to be made from chainmail. Several tribes in Mexico and Peru use similar knitted masks as face protection against the weather.

The version used here covers more of the face than an ordinary knitted mask, since the intention of a burglar would be total disguise. This mask can be adapted for different characters, such as the cat shown below, which has been made from bits of yarn and has had ears added.

k1, p1. (85sts).

Next dec row: k1, k2tog (k16, k2tog tbl, k1, k2tog) 3 times, k16, k2tog tbl,

MATERIALS

- Two 3oz/50g balls black double knitting wool

- pair each of needles size 3/ 3¼mm and 5/4mm

- tapestry needle for sewing up

Abbreviations

k – knit; p – purl; st(s) – stitch(es); st.st. – stockinette stitch; tog – together; tbl – through back of loop; dec – decrease; inc – increase; alt – alternate.

Preparation

Using smaller needles, cast on 98sts.
Work 26 rows in k1. p1. rib.
Change to larger needles.
Work 2 rows in st. st.
Next row: k39, k2tog, k16, k2tog tbl, k to end.
Next row: Purl.
Next row: k38, k2tog, k16, k2tog tb1, k to end. (94sts).
Continue in st.st. for another 13 rows.
Next row: work to last 10sts, leave these on a safety pin.
Repeat this row once. (74sts remain on the needle.)
Dec 1st at each end of next 2 alt. rows. (70sts).
Work straight in st.st. for 19 rows.
Inc. 1st at each end of next 5 alt. rows. (80sts)
Work 1 row.
Cast on 11sts at end of next 2 rows. (102)sts.
Next row: (k1, k2tog, k20, k2tog tbl) twice, k2tog, (k2tog, k20, k2tog tb1, k1) twice. (93sts).
Next and following alt. rows: purl.
Next row: k1, k2tog (k18, k2tog tb1, k1p1, k2tog) 3 times, k18, k2tog tb1,

k1. (77sts).
Next dec row has 14 sts between decreases.
Next dec row has 12 sts between decreases.
Continue in this way until 13sts remain.
Purl 1 row.
Next row: k1 (k2tog, k1) 4 times. (9sts).
Break yarn and thread through

remaining sts, draw up and fasten off.
Sew up head seam using tapestry needle.
Using smaller needles with right side of work facing, pick up and knit 78sts evenly along face edge including the sts. previously left on safety pins.
Work 7 rows in k1, p1, rib. Bind off in ribbing.
Sew up neck seam.

TIP

- You can create a cat by adding fur-fabric ears to the knitted mask. Then use face paints to make a nose and whiskers. You can also make the whiskers from paper.

HAT MASKS

A hat can be used to make a whole head mask with lots of long straggly hair. The Zambians make a woven straw hat with a face piece of the same material attached to the front. There are many ways in which you can make hat masks, and here are two examples. The possibilities for variations are numerous, and you will want to use your own ideas to adapt and change these masks.

NATURAL HAT MASK

Preparation

1. Measure the inside of the hat and cut a piece of linen tape to that length plus 1in/1.5cm. Lay the muslin out; make sure it is not creased. Place the face template over it, about 6in/15cm from the top. Pencil in the outline of the eyes and mouth. Remove template, and paint in the outlines with fabric paints or crayons. Leave to dry.

2. Lay out the linen tape. Put glue along a stretch of tape the same length as the top of the muslin face piece. Glue the tape to the right side of the muslin, and press well down. Turn the tape and face piece over.

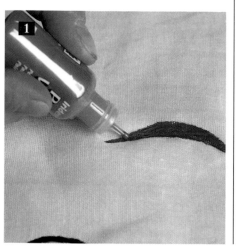

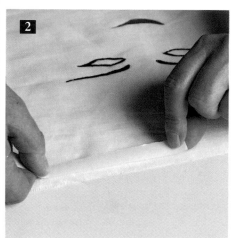

3. Cut lengths of raffia about 18in/45cm long. It is best to glue the raffia to the tape in stages – about 8in/20cm of tape at a time. Put a little glue onto the tape, stick the end part of a bunch of raffia to it, and press it firmly down. When gluing the raffia in place, make sure some of it overlaps the edge of the muslin face piece. You might need to hold the raffia and tape in place with masking tape in order to make it really secure.

NATURAL HAT MASK

4. Spread more glue on top of the linen tape and raffia when the entire length has been covered. Cut another piece of linen tape, the same length as the original, and put it on top of the raffia and muslin. Press down hard and leave to dry. You might like to staple the raffia in place, through the fabric tape, to give extra strength.

5. Lay the raffia wig and the face on the inside of the hat, making sure the face is at the front. Use masking tape to hold in place. Now sew it in place with needle and thread.

Try the mask on. You can cut the raffia hair shorter and thread wooden beads into it if you want. If the stitching and tape show through, the top of the hat and the sides can be decorated with a hat band of raffia.

TIPS

■ You could make the carnival mask without the muslin face and make the wig go all the way around the head. Or you could paint the wearer's face (see face painting, page 32).

■ If you are unable to find a straw hat, make the Halloween hat (see page 64) from appropriately colored board, and glue the wig to the inside of it.

CARNIVAL HAT MASK

Preparation

1. Make this wig in the same way as for the natural mask above, following 1–5. At step 1 paint the face in bright colors. At step 3 use the ribbons, ribbons, tapes, and string to make a mixed wig. Or you could make a wig using thin strips of different-colored crepe paper.

2. Thread a selection of beads and buttons into the hair. If the stitching and linen tape show through, you can decorate the hat with a hat band of different ribbons, string, and beads.

MATERIALS

- straw hat

- white muslin or net 9in × 14in/ 23cm × 35cm

- basic face mask template; see page 119

- selection of colored ribbons, fabric tapes, foil tapes, colored string for the hair

- crepe paper (optional)

- wooden and plastic beads, buttons in lots of colors (optional)

- 1¼in/3cm-wide linen tape 5ft/ 1.5m long

- fabric paints or crayons

- double-sided tape

- masking tape

- all-purpose glue

- stapler (optional)

- needle and thread

- pencil

- scissors

Leo The Lion

Children love to roar behind this full head lion mask. Easy to make from flat board, the lion becomes three-dimensional at the very end. It can be adjusted to fit various head sizes.

Preparation

1. Lay out the large sheet of beige paper horizontally. Draw a light pencil line down the middle of the paper from top to bottom. Having enlarged the main part of the template, lay it over the paper so that the pencil line is half-way between the eyes. Draw around the features. Cut out the eyes and mouth and make the ear slits.

MATERIALS

■ whole head lion template; see page

■ stiff beige or light brown paper 28in × 11in/70cm × 28cm (the grain running down the shorter side)

■ another shade of brown stiff paper 4in × 12in/10cm × 30cm

■ stiff white drawing paper 5in × 4in/12cm × 10cm

■ colored paper in black, beige and white

■ brown and pink paint and brushes

■ tape

■ glue

■ paper clips

■ craft knife and scissors

■ pencil and ruler

2. Place the chin template on the white paper and the ears and nose on the brown paper. Draw around them and cut them out. Score (see techniques, page 16) the sides of the nose along the line indicated on the template. Carefully bend them back to make flaps. Apply glue to the flaps, and glue them in place.

3. Gently push the sides toward each other so that the bridge of the nose is slightly raised.

4. Slot the ears into the ear slots, and hold them in place with tape on the back of the mask.

TIP

This method of mask making can be used to make many other animals. To design your own mask, find a photograph of the animal you have chosen, and make a large drawing of its most important features. Superimpose the tube shape onto this, then trace the features, and you will have the basis of the new mask.

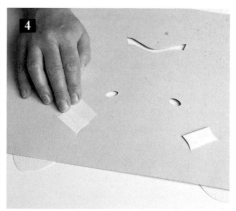

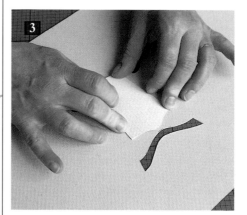

5. Make the hair with the three colored papers. You will need lots of hair in various lengths and thicknesses – a lion can be quite unkempt! Take a piece of paper, score, and fold a line about ½in/1cm from the left edge to make the sticking strip. Cut strips between ⅛in-¼in/ 3mm-7mm wide across the paper from the fold. Curl the thicker strips (see techniques section, page 16).

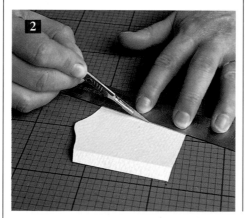

6. Make short white straight hair, and glue it to the chin. Fold back the sticking strip so that it is hidden beneath the hair. Apply glue to the side away from the hair. Glue the chin to the lion.

7. Accentuate the facial features with the paint. He might need a pink nose and lines around the eyes.

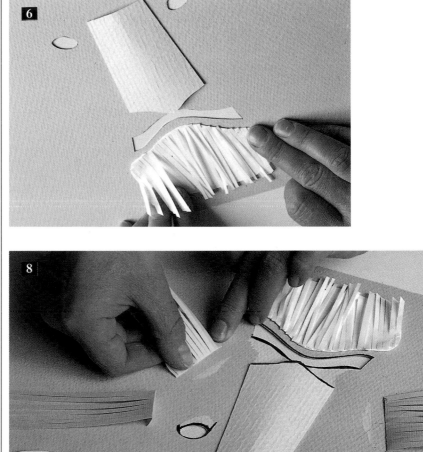

8. Attach the rest of the hair to the lion. Put short pieces along the top of the head and longer pieces down the side of the face. Make the very long pieces go right over the top of the head and down the back. Add some shorter pieces to the back if desired.

9. Bend the mask around the head of the wearer, and fasten it into shape with paper clips at the top or bottom. Take it off and stand it on the table. You can staple the back of the head in place, or, if the mask is to be used by different people, use the paper clips so that the fastening can vary according to the size of the head.

HORSE HEAD MASK

The stylized horse head has been turned into a mask by using very simple paper engineering techniques. As with other designs in the book, the basic characteristics of the animal have been closely observed and incorporated into the pattern. All the lines have been simplified, and other animals can be created in this way – particular attention should be paid to ears, the width of the head, and the nose. The eyes will need great care – in this example it has not been possible to cut the eye holes in the right place, so small holes have been pierced to suit the wearer.

Preparation

1. Trace the pattern from the template section and enlarge it. Draw the pattern on the wrong side of the brown board, and cut out, taking particular care when cutting around the ears and the tabs.

2. Now mark all the lines to be scored and the position of the slots for the tabs. This can be done at each end of the slot by piercing the board with a pin or similar sharp instrument. Score all the lines – if the board is very thick, it will be necessary to cut through part of it – see techniques section, page 16. On the head part, gently bend the curve between the ears. Bend the side pieces from the outer edge of the ear to the nose and also the neck edge to the outer ear. The scored line from the inner edge of the ear to the nose should only be gently creased to give additional shaping to the mask. On the neck part of the mask bend all the scored lines.

3. Check that the position of the slots is correct by aligning the mask parts; adjust as necessary. Then cut the slots. If the board is thick it will be necessary to enlarge the slot slightly. It is better that the slot be tight, as it can always be enlarged. Now cut out the eyes as indicated on the template – note that a very small area has been cut away. Score the small curved lines, and bend the two parts to the inside. Hold the two cut edges together with a piece of tape on the wrong side. Assemble the two parts – head and neck. Slot head sides together and then the head top. On the neck part, work from the top, being careful to align the lower tab before pushing the upper tab into position. Now join the two parts, making sure that the tabs slot in firmly.

4. Cut a strip of fur fabric for the mane, which will fit from the top of the head to the bottom of the neck. Turn under one edge very slightly, and glue this down – it will make the edge of the fur fabric stand up in a most realistic way. Apply glue down the center of the neck from the top of the head, and glue on the "mane." Hold in place until the glue dries.

Cut another piece of fur fabric to positon between the ears, and, using the same method, glue it in place. This piece may require some hairdressing! If fur fabric is not available, use various papers, such as thin colored, crepe, and translucent papers, glue in layers and cut into narrow strips. This is the same method described in greater detail on page 102 for the Lion mask.

5. Finally pierce the two holes marked on the lower jaw, and thread the elastic through these holes. Tie so that the jaw is held in and looks horse-like rather than cow-like! If it is difficult to see through the horse's eyes, extra eye holes can be pierced.

MATERIALS

- horse head template, page ▉▉

- two sheets brown mat board (minimum size 24in × 16½in/ 60cm × 42cm)

- pencil and ruler

- craft knife and scissors

- cutting mat or cardboard

- bone folder (if available)

- fur fabric of a suitable color or light-weight papers

- elastic

ASTRONAUT MASK

This mask has a very simple shape but takes quite a long time to make, since it is constructed in two halves. The decoration is quite simple, and the materials required are readily obtainable. It will be necessary to refer to the American Indian Mask in the previous chapter; see page 89 for detailed instructions on papier-mâché making. In this chapter one very simple method of making a mold will be explained. There are other ways, and is hoped you may wish to investigate them.

The mold has been made by piling screwed-up newspaper onto a flat plastic-covered board and taping the pieces so that they stay in position. The shape into which the newspaper pieces are placed is decided by taking a few basic measurements – overall height, width, and depth. If there are any curves, look carefully where these occur, and use the tape to create the right shape.

When you are satisfied that the overall appearance is correct, cover the mold with clear plastic – this will provide a smooth surface on which to lay the strips. Put a thin layer of petroleum jelly over the surface, then you are ready to start putting on the newspaper strips. The first layer may be a little awkward, but if you use long strips it will help. Making the second layer go in the opposite direction will help you to keep the layers even and will add to the strength.

Preparation

1. Because the mask sits on the shoulders, it will be necessary to measure from the shoulder to the top of the head to ascertain the height measurement. The width is measured across from ear to ear. When working out the depth measurement be sure to remember that you should halve it, since the mask is made in two halves. The depth is measured from the back of the head to the front. All the measurements should be generous, as the finished mask has no openings and simply slips over the head of the wearer.

Roughly mark out the dimensions on the board, and start piling up the newspapers. Do not try to make a cube – the head is rounded! As the pile grows it may be necessary to tape it down as you go along. When you are satisfied with the shape, cover it with plastic – some old plastic bags will serve the purpose.

MATERIALS
■ plastic-covered foundation board for the mold
■ old newspapers
■ sheet of thin plastic
■ masking tape
■ petroleum jelly or similar for release agent
■ all-purpose glue
■ scissors
■ pencil
■ sheet of thin acetate for visor
■ sandpaper
■ silver paint or aluminum foil

2. Using long strips of newspaper, cover the mold right down onto the foundation board. Continue to build up the layers until eight layers have been completed. Leave in a warm place to dry out thoroughly.

3. Carefully lift the half mask off the mold, and set aside until you have completed the second half. Do not worry if the two halves are not absolutely identical.

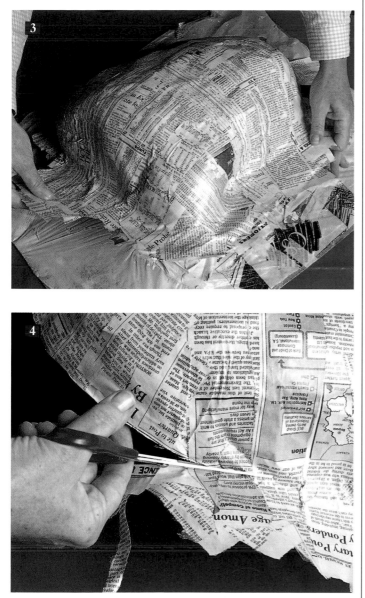

4. Cut away the edge of the mask, which was on the foundation board, including the neck area, and then hold the two halves together to see how well they fit. If necessary, trim away extra bits until the halves touch all around, as much as possible. Small gaps can be covered when the two pieces of the mask are joined.

5. Now cut out the window for the visor in one of the halves. This should be almost as wide as the face and extend from mid-forehead to mid-chin.

6. Tape the two halves together and carefully try on the mask. Join with three or four layers of newspaper strips. At the same time, bind all the cut edges. Leave to dry.

TEMPLATES

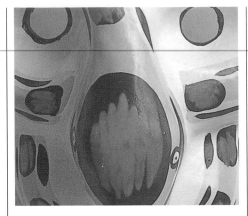

These templates are to be used as the basis for the mask patterns in the project section of the book. They are all labeled and have page references, so that you will know which is which.

Because every face is different it is not possible to give a universal pattern for every style of mask, so you will have to tailor the mask to fit your needs. A well fitting mask should feel comfortable, and the wearer should be able to see through the eye holes without difficulty. With an eye mask, for instance, the position of the wearer's cheek bones will influence the depth of the mask. Some people have eyes wide apart, and others have a pronounced bridge to the nose. You should be aware of these factors when tailoring the mask to fit.

To begin with, it is suggested that you trace the pattern onto stiff paper and try it on the face. Cut or extend this basic shape where necessary, and

in this way you will be able to personalize the patterns. You will soon become accomplished at altering where necessary.

Some of the templates are not shown full size. Any alterations to these will need to be made after the pattern has been enlarged. There are two methods of enlarging patterns.

The smaller patterns can be blown up on a photocopier. In some instances the instructions will tell you by what

percentage the pattern should be increased. Otherwise you could ask the advice of the operator of the photocopier.

The second and more time-consuming method of enlarging patterns is by using a grid system. Trace the pattern you wish to enlarge, and draw a frame closely around it. Divide this frame into a number of small squares. On another piece of tracing paper draw another frame, which will be big enough to contain the enlarged pattern. Divide this second frame into the same number of squares as the first frame with the pattern. Now, transfer the pattern to the second frame by methodically marking points on the grid as the lines from the pattern cross over the squares. Finally join all the marks, and the pattern will be ready.

7. Cut the acetate so that it overlaps the window by ½in/1cm, and stick it in place with small pieces of masking tape and newspaper.

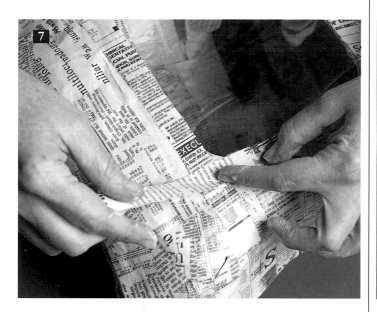

8. Make a border around the window with string covered by two or three layers of papier-mâché.

9. Use sandpaper to smooth away any noticeable bumps, which may have occurred particularly around the join.

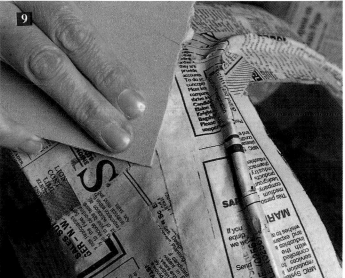

10. Paint with two coats of paint, carefully avoiding the visor area.

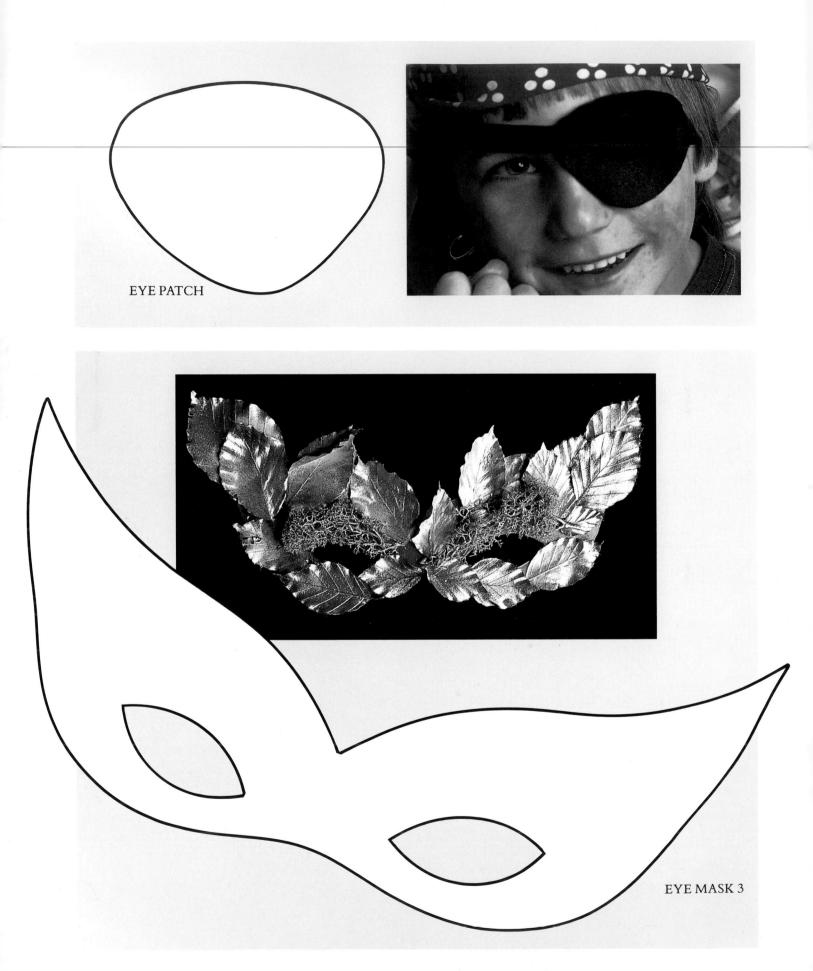

EYE PATCH

EYE MASK 3

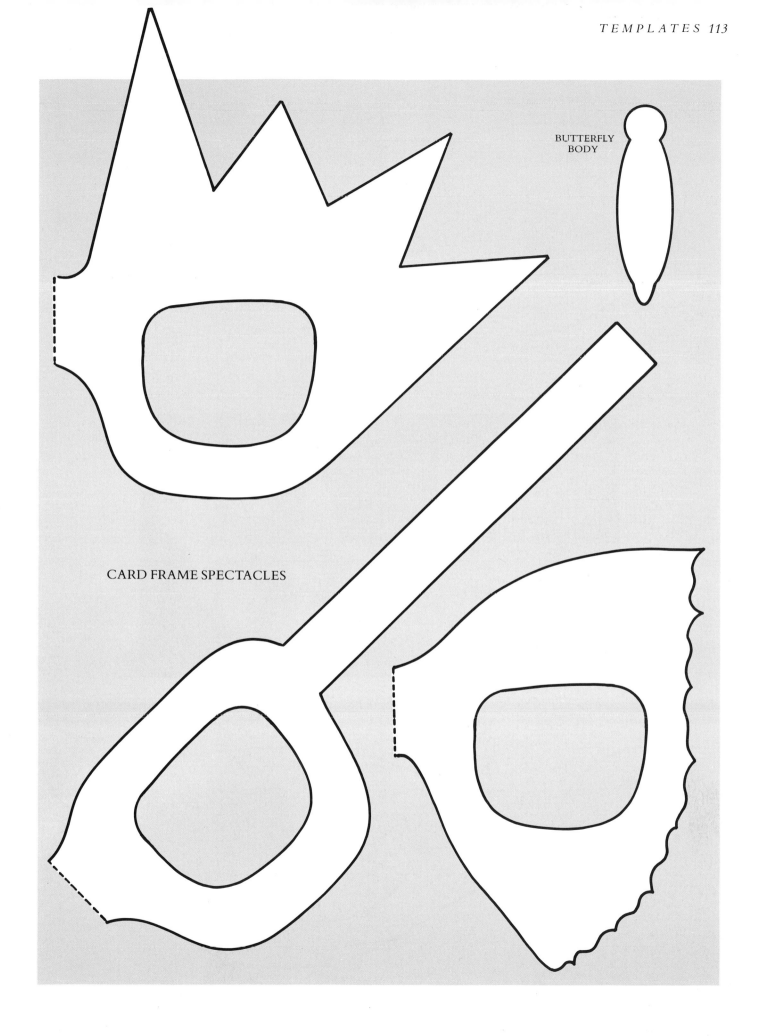

BUTTERFLY
BODY

CARD FRAME SPECTACLES

EYE MASK 1

EYE MASK 2

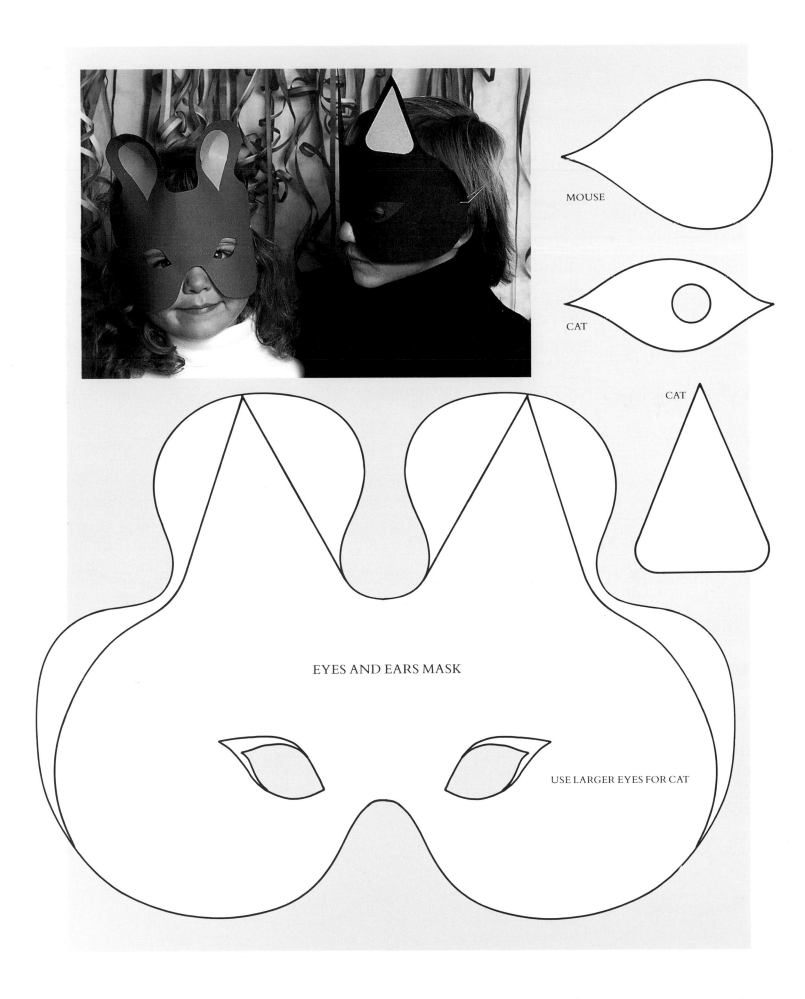

MOUSE

CAT

CAT

EYES AND EARS MASK

USE LARGER EYES FOR CAT

CROWNS AND CORONETS

HARLEQUIN

BASIC FACE MASK

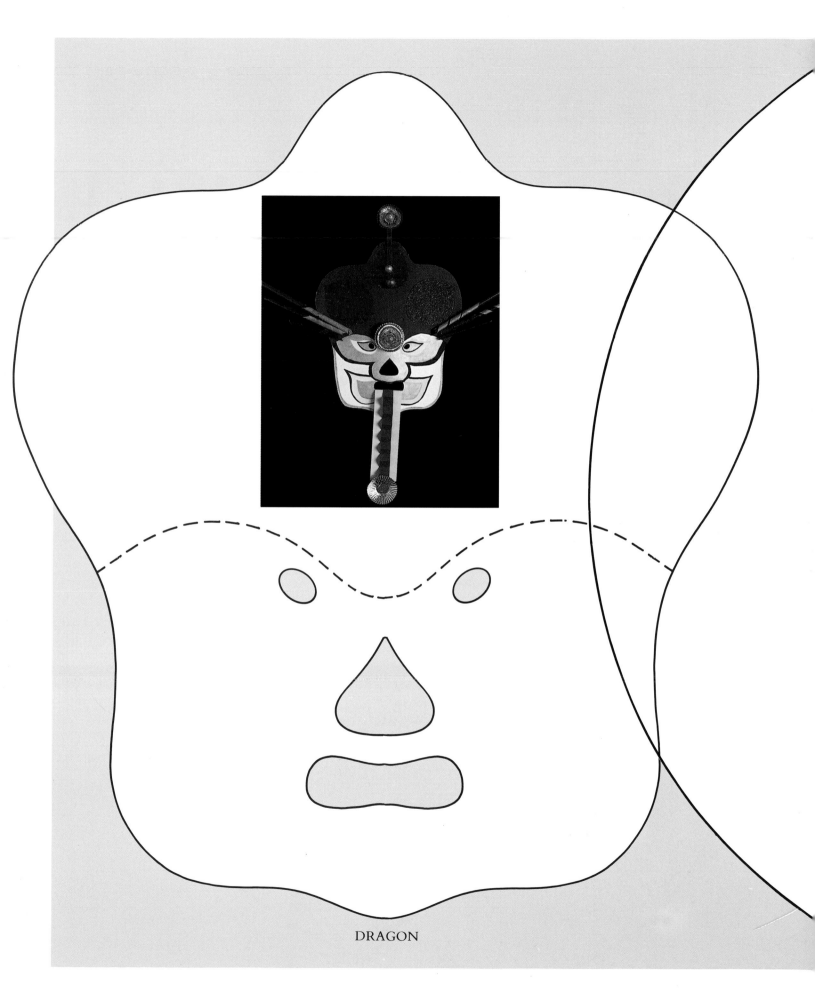

DRAGON

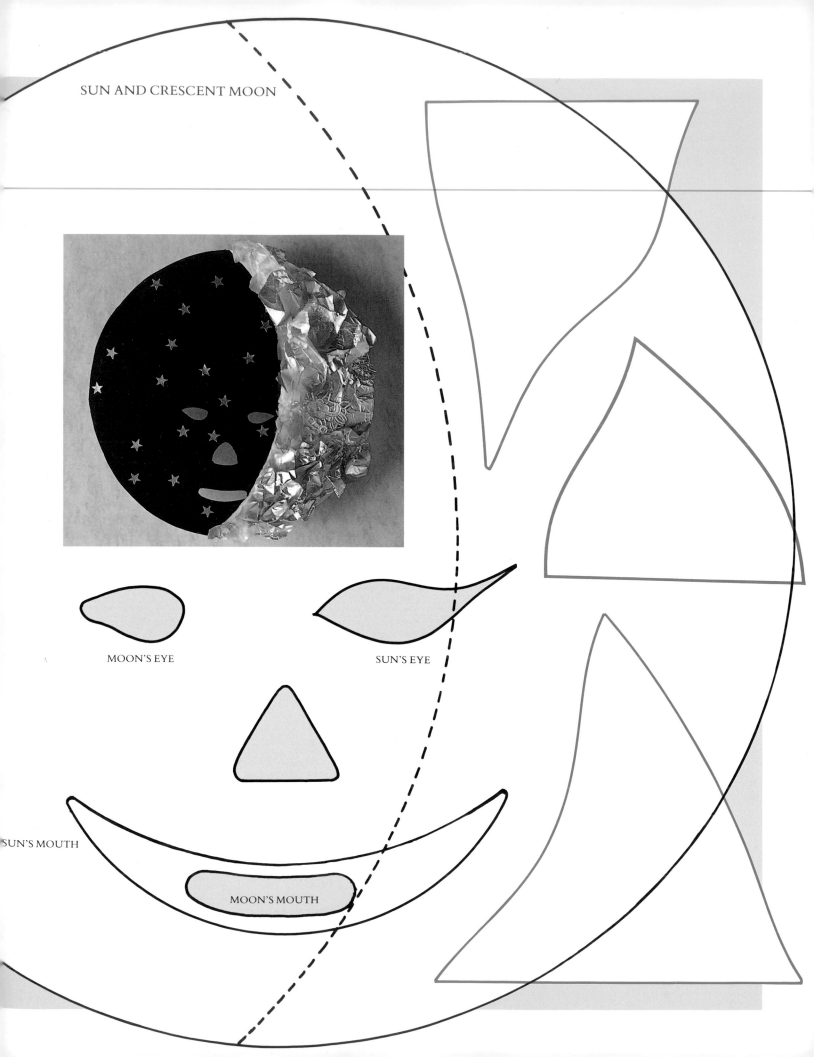

SUN AND CRESCENT MOON

MOON'S EYE

SUN'S EYE

SUN'S MOUTH

MOON'S MOUTH

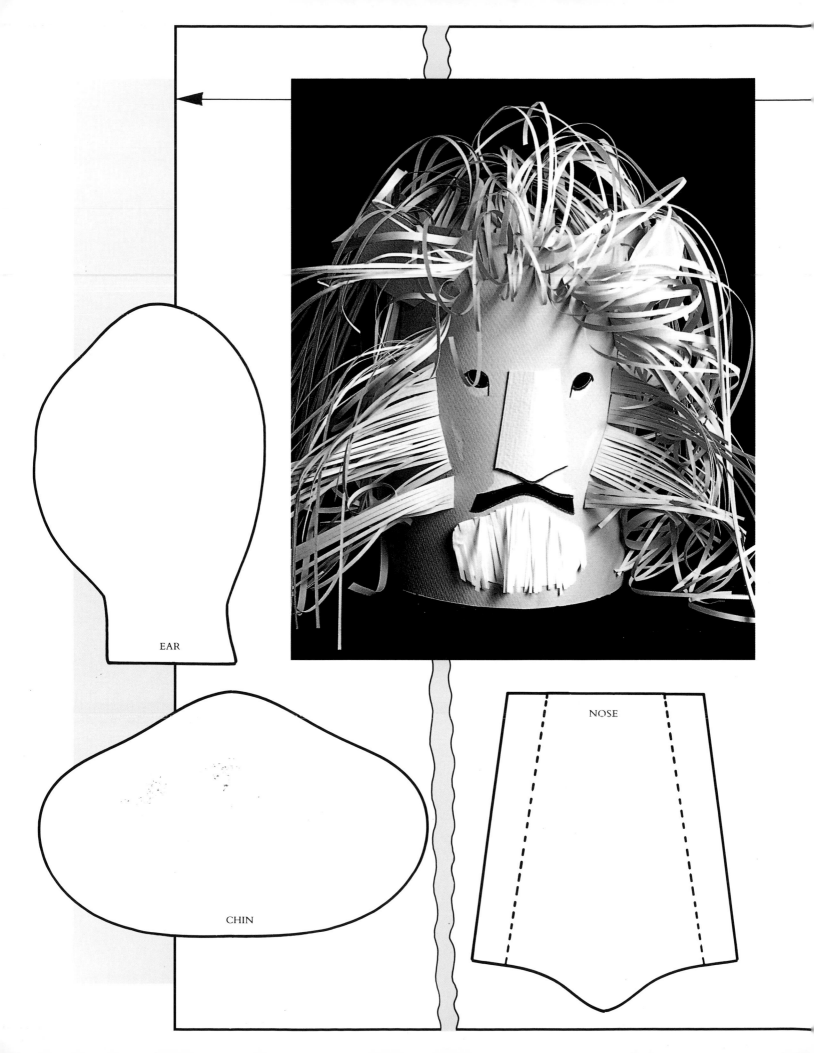

EAR

CHIN

NOSE

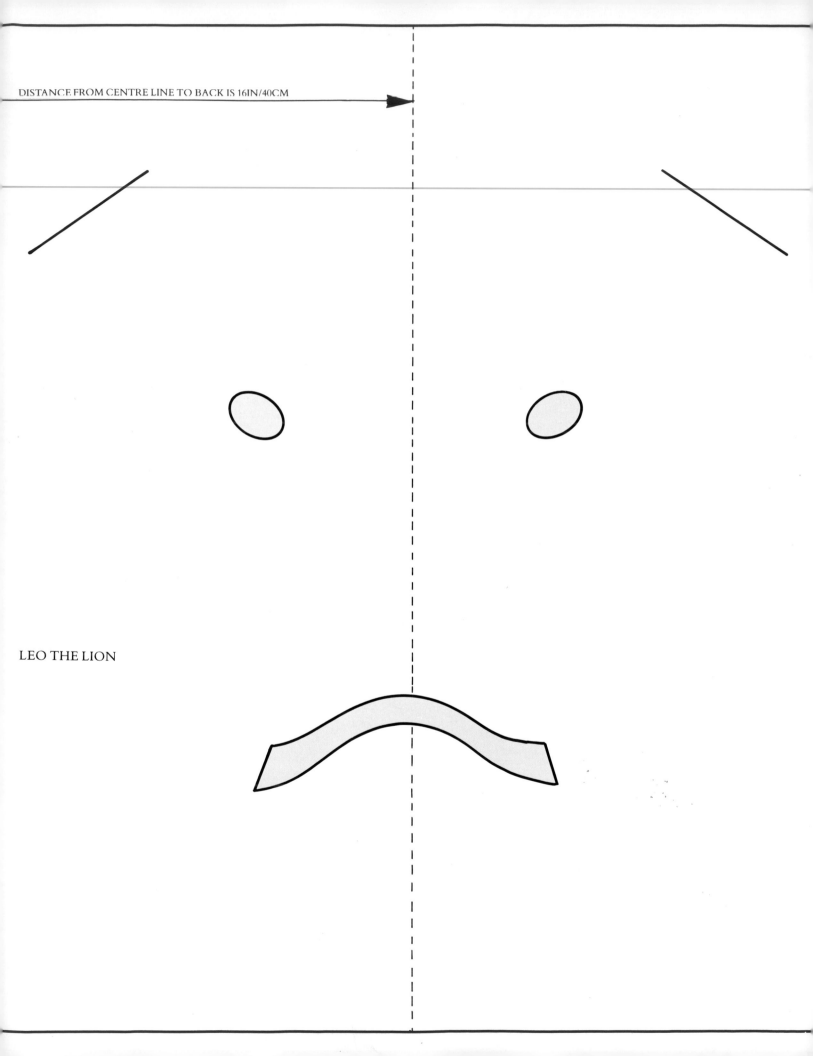

DISTANCE FROM CENTRE LINE TO BACK IS 16IN/40CM

LEO THE LION

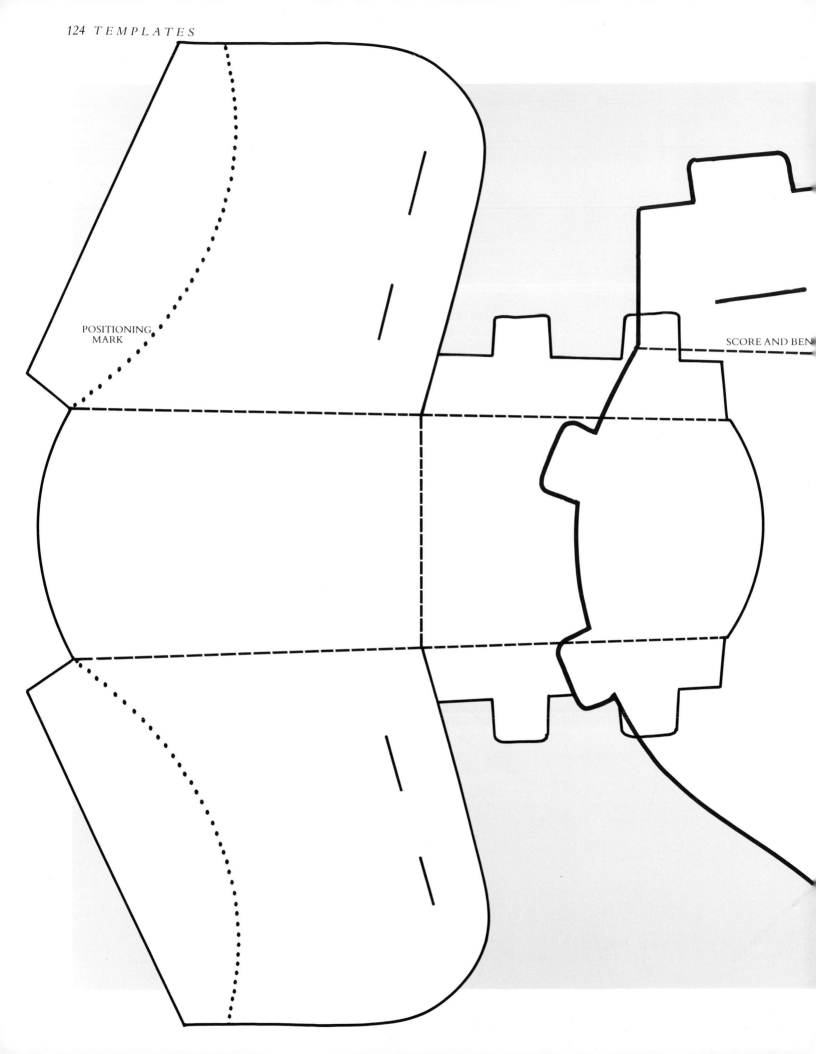

POSITIONING
MARK

SCORE AND BEN

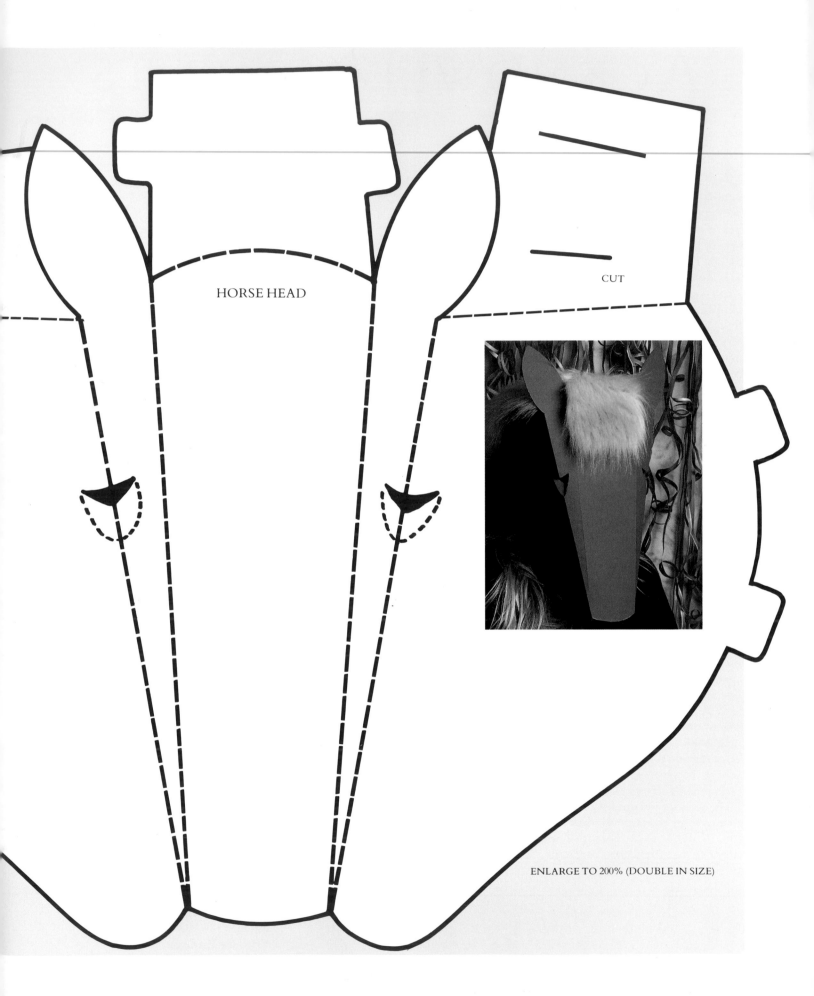

HORSE HEAD

CUT

ENLARGE TO 200% (DOUBLE IN SIZE)

ACKNOWLEDGMENTS

The authors and publishers would like to thank the following companies for their generosity in supplying materials used in the book:
Edding (UK) Ltd.
Pick 'n' Choose
Threadbare
Oakley Fabrics Ltd.
G. F. Smith & Son Ltd.
Maple Textiles
Escapade
Philip & Tacey
For the loan of masks for photography many thanks to:
Zoe Addan
Linda Collins
Edward Levy
Gregory Warren Wilson
   The authors and publishers would also like to thank Julia Cousins, Pitt Rivers Museum; Christine DeCuir, Greater New Orleans Tourist and Convention Commission; Mary Dowling, Horniman Museum; Elizabeth Duff, Play Matters; Nancy Frazier, Museum Insights and Yvonne Schumann, Liverpool Museum. Florence Temko for invaluable assistance with research regarding North American museums, retailers, and background information; Diana Thomson for testing patterns; Marion Elliot for collaborating on the papier-mâché masks; Judith Simons; Marilyn Gasparini; Aurelio Campa; and all those people who showed interest and gave us newspaper cuttings, catalogues, and ideas. Finally, Peter, Caroline, and Jacqueline Frank and George, Madeleine, and Flora Kessler for their support and enthusiasm.
   The authors and publishers acknowledge the origami mask on page 79, designed by Florence Temko, author of many books on paper arts and folk crafts.

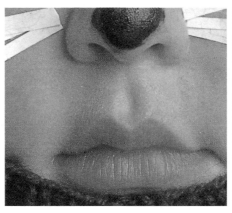

RETAILERS

United Kingdom

Most of the companies listed will be able to send you catalogues. Many of the materials used in this book will be available from your local department store, stationer, or art and craft shop. For specialist supplies consult the Yellow Pages Directory. You could also look in needlecraft and hobby magazines.

Fantasy Fabrics,
Greenmantle, Plough Lane
Christleton, Chester CH3 7BA

Maple Textiles,
188–190, Maple Road
Penge, London SE20 8HT

Oakley Fabrics Ltd.,
8, May St.
Luton, Bedfordshire LU1 3QY

Pick 'n' Choose,
The Craft People, 56 Station Rd.
Northwich, Cheshire CW9 5RB

Threadbare,
Glenfield Pk, Glenfield Rd
Nelson, Lancashire BB12 9PG

Philip and Tacey,
North Way
Andover, Hampshire SP10 5BA

North America

For names of stores that handle mask supplies, consult the Yellow Pages of the phone book under the following headings:
   Artists' Materials
   Costumes – Masquerades and
     Theatrical
   Craft Supplies

Leewards and Michael's are two large chains with many stores carrying a wide selection of handicraft materials. Call their corporate offices for the location of a store near you:

Leewards
100 St. Charles St.
Elgin, IL 60120.
Phone 708/888-5800

Michael's
5931 Campus Circle Dr.
Irving, TX 75063
Phone 214/580-6242

For mail order artists' and school supplies, ask for a catalogue from:

Dick Blick
P.O. Box 1267
Galesburg, IL 61401
Phone 800/447-8192 (toll-free)

Daniel Smith
4130 First Ave So.
Seattle, WA 98134
Phone 800/426-6740 (toll-free)

Also look in the small ads of craft magazines.

CREDITS

Models:
Maria Arbiter
Rebecca Dewing
Spencer Dewing
Caroline Frank
Madeleine Kessler
Janice Williamson

If this book has aroused your curiosity and you are interested in looking at historical and ethnic masks, ask at museums near you whether they have collections of masks, and, if they are not on show, whether it would be possible to see them. Anthropological, folkcraft, ethnic, and natural history museums would almost certainly have some masks, and they would be able to tell you what is on show and to help you in other ways. Some museums have collections. Listed below you will find a limited selection of these museums.

UNITED KINGDOM

Liverpool Museum,
William Brown Street
Liverpool L3 8EN

The British Museum,
Great Russell St.
London WC1

The Horniman Museum,
100, London Rd.
London SE23 3PQ

The Museum of Mankind,
6, Burlington Gdns.
London W1

Pitt Rivers Museum,
South Parks Road
Oxford OX1 3PP

UNITED STATES AND CANADA

Glenbow Museum
130 9th Avenue S.E.
Calgary, Alberta T2G 0P3

Field Museum of Natural History
Roosevelt Road at Lake Shore Drive
Chicago, IL 60605

Fowler Museum of Cultural History
University of California at Los Angeles
Los Angeles, CA 90024

Louisiana State Museum
751 Charles St., P.O. Box 2458
New Orleans, LA 70176

Museum of American Folk Art
444 Park Ave South
New York, NY 10016

American Museum of Natural History
Central Park West at 79th St.
New York, NY 10024

Metropolitan Museum of Art
5th Avenue at 82nd St.
New York, NY 10028

Canadian Museum of Civilization
100 Rue Laurier
P.O. Box 3100, Station B
Hull, Quebec J8X 4H2

Mummers Museum
Second St. and Washington Ave
Philadelphia, PA 17147

North Carolina Museum of Art
2110, Blue Ridge Blvd.
Raleigh, NC 27607

Asian Art Museum
Golden Gate Park
San Francisco, CA 94118

Museum of International Folk Art
706 Camino Lejo, P.O. Box 2087
Santa Fe, NM 87504

Seattle Art Museum
Volunteer Park
Seattle, WA 98112

Royal Ontario Museum
100 Queen's Park
Toronto, Ontario M5S 2C6

U.B.C. Museum of Anthropology
University of British Columbia
6393 Northwest Marine Drive
Vancouver, British Columbia
Z6T 1W5

Royal British Columbia Museum
675 Bellevill St.
Victoria, British Columbia V8Z 1X4

Smithsonian Institution
10th St. and Constitution Ave. N.W.
Washington, D.C. 20560

BIBLIOGRAPHY

Alkema, J. A., *Mask Making* (Sterling Publishing Co., N.Y.C.)

Bawden, J., *The Art & Craft of Papier-Mâché* (Mitchell Beazley, London, 1990)

Bihalji-Merin, O., *Masks of the World* (Thames & Hudson, London, 1971)

De la Porte des Vaux, D., *Masques aux quatre saisons* (Editions Fleurus, Paris)

Drew, L., *Haida: Their Art and Culture* (Hancock House, 1982)

Duffek, K., *Bill Reid: Beyond the Essential Form* (University of British Columbia Press, Vancouver, 1986)

Ebin, V., *The Body Decorated* (Thames & Hudson, London, 1979)

Hardy, A., *Mardi Gras Guide* (published annually by Arthur Hardy Enterprises Inc., 4441 Iberville St., New Orleans, LA 70119)

Jonaitis, A., *From the Land of the Totem Poles* ([The N.W. Coast Indian Art Collection at the American Museum of Natural History] pub. American Museum of Natural History, N.Y.C./ British Museum Publications, London, 1988)

Kondeatis, C., *Masks: Ten Amazing Masks to Assemble and Wear* (Pan, London and Sydney, 1987)

Levi-Strauss, C., *Structural Anthropology* (Penguin, London, 1965)

O'Hanlon, M., *Reading the Skin: Adornment, Display and Society among the Wangi* (British Museum Publications, London, 1989)

Pegg, B., *Rites and Riots: Folk Customs of Britain and Europe* (Blandford Press, Poole, Dorset, 1981)

Ray, D. J., *Eskimo Masks* (Univ. of Washington Press, Seattle, 1976)

Rinck, M.-P., *Macquillages pour jouer* (Editions Fleurus, Paris)

Segy, L., *Masks of Black Africa* (Dover Publications, N.Y.C. 1976)

Snook, B., *Making Masks* (Batsford, London, 1972)

Statler, O., *(Introduction) All Japan: The Catalogue of Everything Japanese* (Columb's, London/Quarto, N.Y.C., 1984)

Stewart, H., *Looking at Indian Art of the Northwest Coast* (Douglas and McIntyre, Vancouver and Toronto, 1979)

Teuten, T., *Masks: The Letts Guide to Collecting* (Letts, London, 1990)

Wright, L., *Masks* (Franklin Watts, London, 1989)